To Connie,
The Strength.
The Gaskin Family,
Love Ed Blessings,
Dave Smiot
Col 3:17

The Life and Times of Tucker Pitts

The Life and Times of Tucker Pitts
1957-1963

Douglas Forde Simms

JAMES A. ROCK & COMPANY, PUBLISHERS
FLORENCE • SOUTH CAROLINA

The Life and Times of Tucker Pitts: 1957–1963 by Douglas Forde Simms

JAMES A. ROCK & COMPANY PUBLISHERS — established 1973

JAMES A. ROCK & COMPANY, PUBLISHERS

The Life and Times of Tucker Pitts: 1957–1963
copyright ©2009 Douglas Forde Simms

Special contents of this edition copyright ©2009
by James A. Rock & Co., Publishers

All applicable copyrights and other rights reserved worldwide. No part of this publication may be reproduced, in any form or by any means, for any purpose, except as provided by the U.S. Copyright Law, without the express, written permission of the publisher.

This is a work of fiction. Names, characters, places and incidents either are the product of the author's imagination or are used fictitiously. Any resemblance to actual events, locales, organizations, or persons, living or dead, is entirely coincidental and beyond the intent of either the author or the publisher.

Note: Product names, logos, brands, and other trademarks occurring or referred to within this work are the property of their respective trademark holders.

Address comments and inquiries to:

James A. Rock & Company, Publishers
900 South Irby, #508
Florence, South Carolina 29501

E-mail:
jrock@rockpublishing.com   lrock@rockpublishing.com
Internet URL: www.rockpublishing.com

Trade Paperback ISBN: 978-1-59663-695-8

Library of Congress Control Number: 2008926164

Printed in the United States of America

First Edition: 2009

In Memoriam

Three artists featured in
The Life and Times of Tucker Pitts: 1957–1963
have passed away since writing the book.
While saddened by their death,
I celebrate their life.

Marv Johnson
October 15, 1938–May 16, 1993

Ray Peterson
April 23, 1935–January 25, 2005

Chuck Rio
1929–September 19, 2006

Acknowledgments

Praise God from whom all blessings flow—first, last, and always.

This book is dedicated to all the pioneers of Rock 'n Roll, Rhythm & Blues, and Motown. Their gifts continue to bring a never ending joy to millions of fans.

The author especially wishes to thank Mr. William "Bill" Cooper, Dr. Mark "Tiger" Edmonds, Professor Emeritus of English, St. Leo University, Mr. Robert Henry, friend and Screenwriter, Mr. Gordy Singer, friend and Personal Manager, and Mr. Ed Healy for their selfless guidance throughout the Tucker Pitts project. Their contributions were invaluable. I am also grateful to those whom I've forgotten to mention.

I am most thankful to my wife, JoAnn, whose constant encouragement kept me focused and at the computer.

Contents

Introduction xi

Prologue 1

CHAPTER ONE
Tucker Pitts 3
   Profile: Carl Gardner—the Coasters 8

CHAPTER TWO
Hannah and the Bowling Alley Beast 13
   Profile: Arlene Smith—the Chantels 19

CHAPTER THREE
Timing is Everything 25
   Profile: Chuck Rio—the Champs 31

CHAPTER FOUR
The Peg Leg Man 35
   Profile: Johnny Maestro—the Crests 44

CHAPTER FIVE
"Not in your lifetime, pork-o" 49
   Profile: Jimmy Beaumont—the Skyliners 57

CHAPTER SIX
When You Wish Upon a Star 63
   Profile: Tony Carlucci—the Impalas 71

CHAPTER SEVEN
A Siren's Song 75
   Profile: Johnny Farina—Santo & Johnny 85

CHAPTER EIGHT
Down For the Count 89
   Profile: Marv Johnson 98

CHAPTER NINE
"Camping? Really? But what if I break a nail?" 103
  Profile: Ray Peterson 112

CHAPTER TEN
The Butterfly Phenomenon 117
  Profile: Gladys Horton—The Marvelettes 125

CHAPTER ELEVEN
Mary Elise Giambone 133
  Profile: Joey Dee—the Starliters 144

CHAPTER TWELVE
The Boys of Avon Avenue 151
  Profile: Albert "Diz" Russell—the Orioles 168

CHAPTER THIRTEEN
"Thank you and good night." 173
  Profile: Cathy Jean—the Roommates 187

CHAPTER FOURTEEN
Tucker's Pitt Stop 191
  Profile: Lesley Gore 204

Epilogue 215

Introduction

For some, it is the gossamer world of Fine Art in all its convolutions—the Abstractionists, the Impressionists, the interpretations, and the explanations. Some might even prefer Opera with their artwork. It goes better with the champagne and shrimp salad. Faw, faw, faw, faw, faw.

Others would argue that bowling a few frames on Friday nights, with a longneck beer bottle peeking out of their back pocket and wincing to a George Jones tune, makes all the crap-ola they put up with during the week at the foundry worth it.

I met music on Christmas morning, 1956, and I don't mean just a casual meeting, either. I mean a face to face, head on collision. The kind that leaves stars circling around your head in a wobbly orbit. The kind where tiny plus signs replace your eyes.

The Christmas gift came wrapped in silver foil and tied with a blue, velvet ribbon. It was heavy and comforting, as if I held the Holy Grail. I was holding 78-rpm (revolutions per minute) records in my lap. A lot of them. More than I had ever seen much less owned. The one on top had a purple label with a likeness of The Capitol Building in Washington, D.C. on it. It was a song called "Be Bop A Lula" by Gene Vincent and the Bluecaps. Underneath was a record by Carl Perkins entitled, "Blue Suede Shoes." There was "Young Love," by Sonny James, and more.

Prior to that morning, my musical tastes ranged from Patti Page, Peggy Lee, the TV show "Your Hit Parade," and the show tunes I sang as a regular cast member on the Sunday morning, NBC-TV series "The Children's Hour."

The elements of this new music stirred up unfamiliar and confusing emotions. They combined powerful, new rhythms and soulful voices to produce a spiritual and visceral sound. It was raw, daring, and wonderful. It was the sound of the voices in harmony that paralyzed me; like a deer frozen in a car's headlights.

Then, suddenly, it was 1989. For more than 30 years, I willingly indulged my harmony habit with vocal oriented groups ranging from The Five Satins, to Three Dog Night, to the Startones, the a cappella group I recorded with in 1962.

I was asked to contribute a celebrity interview column to the international music and nostalgia newspaper, *Blue Suede News.* The Chairperson of The Foundation for the Love of Rock and Roll, a now defunct charitable organization whose mission was to build a retirement home for aging Rockers, said the interviews would help promote and illuminate the artist's and the Foundation's goal. They would make available some of the "Pioneers" of Rock 'n Roll and Motown for interviews. For the next several years, I had the honor and privilege of meeting and interviewing some of the most influential recording artists and some of the nicest people of the '50s, '60s, and early '70s.

One overcast, boring Saturday afternoon, several years after *Blue Suede News* closed their doors, and the "FLR&R" disbanded, I gathered together the interview manuscripts of my old column, *"A Chat with an Old Friend,"* and placed them in chronological order from 1957-1971. When I originally conducted and wrote the interviews, the artists were made available to me on a random basis, so I never read the finished interviews in any order—until that gray, rainy Saturday.

An exciting 22-chapter panorama of American Pop music history and culture propelled itself off the pages unlike anything I had read before; and it was narrated by those directly in the arena. My cassette tapes had caught it all.

Throughout the ensuing years, many friends, family, and some of the artists themselves, nudged me to have the interviews published in a book. I resisted. My rationale was that celebrity interviews were a fairly common occurrence and quickly forgotten. The prevailing attitude was on to the next! I didn't want to diminish them. If I *were* to submit them for publication, I wanted to add another dimension that could make the history indelible and relatable.

Many of these artists and I had things in common, some growing up not far from where I lived my teenage years. Their music, voices, lyrics, whatever the heavenly combination, guided me into a whole new world. I lived it, I breathed it, and I survived it. And I was blessed that these artists, and their songs, steered me through adolescent heartache, and helped me navigate some choppy teenage waters. Their music provided background, nuance, and filled in the blanks. I digress.

Sometimes I got confused when listening to the vocal and a cappella groups of the '50s and '60s. Sometimes, they sounded like the boldest of church choirs, resonating with drama, and resounding with the sweetness of the Holy Spirit. They were their own orchestra. Sometimes they roared and wailed; sometimes they tickled—but always with respect. When I first heard Billy Ward and the Dominoes brilliant vocal arrangement of Hoagy Carmichael's, "*Star Dust,*" I thought there could never be another song that beautiful. And when I closed my eyes and listened, I was transported into a Cathedral.

Church music was a large part of my life, and I loved the choir. The choir's harmonies were so textured and fluid that they kept me enchanted, off balance, barely leaving me time to catch my breath. The emerging Rhythm & Blues (R&B) and vocal Rock 'n Roll groups had the identical effect. There were four and five part harmonies in some groups; the voices ranged from Bass, Alto, 2nd Tenor, 1st Tenor. The voices in harmony, especially tight harmonies, were an amusement park of sound. Sometimes the good ones brought me to my knees in prayer. I told you I was captivated.

It was that romance, that seduction of sound that I wanted to weave into a story. It dawned on me that it might be neat having the reader tag alongside an 11-year old boy as he "comes-of-age" in that frenzied, yet simple time; and then end each chapter with a brief interview with the recording artist noted in the story.

Enter Tucker Pitts, a plump, doe-eyed adolescent with an engaging smile and a quick wit. When his interests turn from Saturday morning cartoons to the Top-10 Music Charts, it heralds the beginning of a young boy's explosive journey into an uncertain future, a nuclear showdown, and the emergence of a backbeat.

The sixteen years between 1957 and 1973 were defined by some of the most dramatic and soul altering events in American history. The cultural, political, social, moral, and scientific landscape had downshifted from the high speed drive of back-to-back wars, returning to a slower, simpler and more prosperous time. "Rosie the Riveter" had returned home and exchanged a lunch pail for a frilly apron.

Then televisions mushroomed in homes across the country; satellites were launched into outer space, commercial jet travel began, and technology was fully unleashed in the Twentieth Century.

The music took on a backbeat and guided a revolution.

The Life and Times of Tucker Pitts is a novel covering the period from 1957-1963. It is the presentation of those dizzying times seen mostly through the eyes of the precocious Tucker, his seven-year old sister, Blanche, and his parents, Farmer, and Vienna Pitts, and an assortment of "way out" characters.

It is through Tucker's life growing up in the shadows of Manhattan that we experience what it was like to ride through those chaotic decades in the big finned cars, watch Jack Benny on TV, survive a nuclear missile crisis, a presidential assassination, and a war in the jungles tucked far away from civility.

Bob Dylan warned, "The times, they are a changing."

The Life and Times of Tucker Pitts is the story of a young boy's journey into adulthood told in apple pie slices. Join him as he comes of age, stumbles head on into a decade of whirlwind events, and becomes a casualty in an explosive development in popular music called Rock 'n Roll. Maybe no other time in our entire history had so many things changed so fast, and in so many different directions.

The Life and Times of Tucker Pitts offers up a deep dish slice of life, served warm, a bite at a time, in a recipe of simple days gone nuclear.

It's like when Grand Funk Railroad sings, "If you want to make the scene, come along baby, and step into my time machine."

Professor Emeritus of English, St. Leo University, and author, Dr. Mark Edmonds *(Longrider, The Ghost of Scootertrash Past,* and *The Lonesome Lowdown Long-gone Outbound Scootertrash Blues)* says.

Tucker's tales will make you laugh, and they will bring you to nostalgic sorrowful tears of longing. His story not only provokes memories, it will make you ponder and wonder about all kinds of things between back then and now. The interviews will do the same as they answer a few questions we've all wondered about.

And for the young readers, this is the definitive guide to an important era in both American and musical history, all through the eyes of Tucker Pitts. This is the kind of book you read out loud to the people around you, that you pass on to folks who you shared some of the memories with that you hand to your kids.

Prologue

In the blistering summer heat of 1945, while millions of people popped champagne corks and hurled tons of confetti onto streets already littered with celebrants; while Soldiers, and Sailors, and Marines, and Airmen bowed deeply, acknowledging a grateful nation, 31-year old Farmer Pitts paced nervously back and forth in the waiting room in St. Barnabas Hospital lighting up one cigarette after another.

In an operating room one floor above, his wife, Vienna, grunted one last time, and onto the world's stage emerged its newest actor, Tucker Pitts.

As the story goes, baby Tucker was one of 11 births that day, eight girls and three boys. And up until lunchtime, on his second day of life, he was just a run of the mill, wrinkled, pink-skinned infant with a finely advanced set of lungs—just one of the boys. No different from the others, boys and girls alike. All had ten fingers and toes. All gurgled and cooed. All had the right parts and they worked as intended.

During his noon feeding, while Vienna cradled him in her arms, a red welt in the shape of the letter "V" appeared in the middle of Tucker's forehead. The mark didn't last long before it faded away, maybe a day or two, but it was long enough to convince everyone that this new life was anointed, that the "V" stood for Victory, and that its revelation, coming on the heels of WWII, was compelling evidence of a spirited messenger.

CHAPTER ONE

Tucker Pitts

May, 1957

Eleven-year old Tucker Pitts was, as his mother liked to say, "Pleasingly plump." He was not exactly fat, but more like a precocious and belly rolling laughing boy with a high pompadour. No one seemed to notice it except for his Aunt Corrine, who could never pass up the opportunity to interrogate him.

"Do you eat because you're hungry or because it TASTES GOOD?" She would growl into his ear at every visit.

With few exceptions, like when Ralphie Amato and his inbred friends rolled him up inside a gym mat and put him naked in the schoolyard, life was good for Tucker. It would be great in fact, if it were not for the talk that the Dodgers and Giants might leave New York for California.

Tucker was hitting close to .300 for his Little League team and was chosen to be the starting catcher in the All-Star game. Best of all, last night he got to stay up late and watch the Friday

Night Fights with his father (complete with his very own bottle of Pepsi and bag of Frito's Corn Chips). He had a slobbering dog named Dorsey, and a pet duck he called Billy Boy.

It was a typical Saturday night and the smells of fried chicken and lima beans still lingered in the kitchen from supper. Good smells Tucker thought, the kind of smells that must saturate Ozzie and Harriet's home.

"Come on, Mom!" Tucker whined, plucking the string on the bakery box. It was time for desert and he suspected there were four Charlotte Rouse inside, their yellow cake piled high with whipped cream. "Can't you put a little zip into the dishes there?"

Vienna Pitts leaned against the kitchen counter and wiped the inside of the cast iron frying pan. "You hold your horses, Tucker, or I'm gonna put some zip into you," she grinned, playfully swatting at her young son with the dishtowel.

Minutes later, the slender Vienna put away the last of the dishes and turned her attention to the white box. Tucker was right. It contained his favorite desert, Charlotte Rouse. She poured a cold glass of milk and put a cardboard bound pastry in front of her son.

Tucker pierced the swirled mountain of whipped cream with his tongue, just as the phone rang in the living room.

"Tucker, it's for you. It's Kerry," his father yelled. Kerry McDonough was Tucker's best friend.

"Oh shi...," Tucker started to blurt out.

"WHAT did you say, Tucker?" his mother asked. "Shoot, ma. Oh, shoot, is what I was going to say." Tucker quickly squeezed out from the kitchen table and scooted toward the only telephone in their house. *Jeez, I'll never get to eat the Charlotte Rouse before Alan Freed comes on. This had better be important,* he thought.

Shortly afterward, Tucker reappeared in the kitchen and breathlessly asked his mother, "Did you know that Wolfie's grandparents were Nazi spies, Mom? They sent coded messages in secret pigeon poop." Wolfgang Rupert lived five homes down the block from Tucker's family and was a playmate of his.

"Who told you that, Tucker?" Vienna asked, nearly choking on a swallow of her coffee.

"Kerry did, just now, Mom! His father had a few too many hi-balls and let it slip. Is it true?" Tucker returned to his pastry before his mother answered.

"Well, yes ... sort of," she sputtered, dabbing at the coffee stream dribbling down her chin. "Don't you dare repeat this, but they were picked up by the FBI as members of a local *Bund.*"

"What did they play, Mom?" Tucker quizzed. "Polkas?"

"Not a band, Tucker, a *Bund.*"

"What's that?"

"There were lots of them around these parts during the war. They were groups of Germans who had sympathies for their homeland, and they gathered together at secret meetings."

"Kind of like the Masons that Daddy belongs to?" Tucker asked.

"Not exactly, kiddo. Wolfie's grandparents kept pigeons on their roof and used them to ferry messages strapped on their legs. And it was a secret pigeon COOP, not poop."

"Oh," Tucker mumbled, temporarily losing interest in the talk of spies in the neighborhood. A thick glob of the rich whipped cream slid out of his mouth, over his bottom lip and plopped onto the Formica. Tucker made quick work of the French pastry and gulped down the remainder of his milk, leaving a white mustache on his upper lip.

"Tucker, I'm running your water. Get ready for your tub," Vienna directed, moving toward the bathroom.

"Yes ma'am, I'll be right there." Tucker had 20-minutes before his favorite radio show came on. Just enough time to take his bath and prepare for the "Rock 'n Roll Party."

No. Life definitely did not get much better than this.

While Tucker tried to float in eight inches of warm bath water, Vienna brought coffee to her husband, who was sitting in an over-stuffed armchair, reading the *Newark Evening News.*

"Anything interesting in the paper, Farmer?" It was her husband's "family" name.

"Yes. Mike Wallace got dumped as the mystery guest from 'What's My Line,'" he answered, a stream of smoke rising from his pipe. "It seems John Daly didn't like him interviewing that ex-gangster Mickey Cohen. He said, 'It would not be in the best of taste for Wallace to be on the show.'"

Tucker's parents settled in for a night of TV as he toweled himself off. Hurriedly, he put on his pajamas, robe and slippers, and ambled into the kitchen.

After yanking open a cabinet drawer and pulling out a pad of paper and a pencil, Tucker grabbed hold of the edge of the wash sink and pulled himself up to the top of the wooden stool. His father recently added an upholstered seat to it for just these occasions, but he still sat too low. No matter how much his mother told him he grew, his head barely popped up over the ridge of the double washtubs.

Tucker stood on the highest rung of the stool, reached over, and grunted as he strained to pull the corrugated metal cover over the open washbasin. He gingerly positioned the radio to maximize reception, tuned it to WINS, and flipped open his legal pad to a clean page.

At the top, he wrote, TOP 10—May 14, 1957, and numbered the blue lines from one to ten. It was Saturday night, 6:29 p.m. and, in one minute, "Alan Freed's Rock 'n Roll Party" started.

Tucker, eager to hear the new countdown, began to fidget and squirm trying to get comfortable. In an attempt to adjust the blue terrycloth bathrobe that poked up uncomfortably beneath him, he grabbed hold of the hem on his robe and yanked upward as hard as he could. The trouble was that he mistook the cuff on his pajama leg for the bathrobe (it was a matching set), and nearly killed himself in a backward flip off the stool.

Embarrassed, but otherwise unruffled, Tucker took advantage of the opportunity and retrieved the thick phone book. After setting it on top of the cushioned seat, he climbed back up the stool and sat on top of it. Alan Freed was just introducing the hilarious new vocal group, The Coasters.

Profile: CARL GARDNER—the Coasters
Interview: May 22, 1990

What is your opinion of the early days of Rock 'n Roll?

"Those were the days of taking. Everybody was ripping everybody off. The Coasters, I would say, was one group that got more money out of the record company than anybody else was. I was very aggressive.

"I remember when I was with The Robins, I went to Las Vegas and I saw all the entertainers, including Billy Eckstine, dressing across the railroad tracks to work in these beautiful clubs.

"I didn't know anything about the mob. I was from the country. You know in those days, the mob probably owned Las Vegas. We were working The Home of the Dancing Waters, I think that's now called Caesar's Palace, and the bosses used to say that if we were too loud, they would throw cans at us because people were gambling.

"The bombs would be going off in the background. The atomic bombs were being tested back then, and we'd look up and there would be big black smoke coming up all over the place.

"So anyway, one day I walked in and said, 'I don't like this that we have to dress across the tracks, and then come up here to work.' I said that if we could work for them, surely they can give us a room in this place. I got mad and I said, 'Listen, man, we didn't come here to mess with your women, or to steal, or do anything but go to work and do what we have to do. Now give me a room in this place.'

"The guy looked at me, and I didn't know that he was a mobster, so he went and got all the bosses together and asked me to say that again. I did. Do you know that they gave us dressing rooms in that place but not a room?

"So, as far as I'm concerned, I integrated Vegas in those days."

What were the early days of Rock 'n Roll like?
"Everybody had their liquor and stuff in the dressing room, drinking and trying to take on this heavy work. It was really Rock 'n Roll slavery, I call it. There was too much work, too many jobs.

"Our managers were behind everything that went down, including the stealing. They were only thinking one way—do this job and give me my twenty percent, and anything else I can steal from you.

"Everybody got rich in those days except the entertainer. Maybe we were making money and didn't know it. You never know things in this business. Sometimes money is hidden through contracts."

What did The Coasters do?
"I do remember going to New Mexico, once. We had a contract for $3000 for one night. The place was so packed that I got mad and said that we were not going on stage unless we got $2000 more. We had a contract for $3000, but I didn't care. I said to the promoter, 'Do you want a riot here?'

"I jacked him up and we got our money that night. Still, five people got killed after the show, and I was talking about a riot because we wouldn't go on. There were Mexicans, Indians, Whites and every nationality you could think of. Somebody had thrown up a chair

THE COASTERS
Featuring Carl Gardner
(Original) Lead Singer

while we were on stage, and the whole place went wild. We had to lock ourselves in the dressing room. After the show, five people lay dead out there.

"The next day the headlines all over the country read, 'COASTERS START RIOT!'"

In its inception, Rock 'n Roll was frightening to many parents. Why do you think that was?

"In those days, it was 'race music.' They didn't want white kids to be affiliated with the kind of stuff we were coming out with, which is OK today. In those times, they didn't appreciate it—kids trying to latch on to that kind of music.

"They called it 'nigger music,' 'hate music,' whatever. In my heart, I didn't believe how they thought about it. I thought, maybe, perhaps, that it was a power source.

"Money is our source, here in America. If we had the power, it would be money. For instance, if you go to New York, in the old days, the Italians ran the city. Now, the Jews run the city. They got more money. They didn't want us to make that rise.

"You have to understand where I'm coming from. You still don't know, truthfully, what was going down in those days. We ran into a lot of racial things on buses going through Alabama.

"There would be a white, Jewish manager on the bus, controlling the bus. He would go into the back of this restaurant in Alabama, and say that he wanted to feed the people on the bus. They told him to, 'Get the hell out of here. We're not gonna feed all them niggers.'

"So what we'd have to do is drive to a supermarket and pick up some cheese, crackers and cold cuts. We'd have our meal on the bus, on the way to the next job, until we could get to a 'black hotel' or places where we could have 'soul food.'

"But on our way down there, we had to bring our own sandwiches. We couldn't eat or stay in good, 'white hotels.'

Carl, what impact did The Coasters have on Rock 'n Roll?

"I think we played a very, very important part in Rock 'n Roll. We did things, which others had not done, or were hard to sell. It's very hard to sell a novelty record. It's very hard to make hits out of novelty tunes. We were successful at doing so.

"We did all types of music with the group, from Pop on down to Rhythm and Blues, and back up to Rock 'n Roll. We've done it all."

Do you feel that the contemporary Rock 'n Roll artists owe the pioneers of the recording industry anything?

"They owe us one hell of a 'Thanks.' Let me put it in another way. In the Bible, God says, 'I am a jealous God. Have no Gods before me.' Jesus was supposedly sent to make Man repent of his sins. I say to you, as far as I'm concerned, I serve God.

"I'm not saying that the pioneers are God but, doggone it, they did find and discover Rock 'n Roll. If it weren't for us, no one would be singing it today. After all, we are the pioneers."

Partial Discography
CARL GARDNER: THE COASTERS
- "Down In Mexico"
- "Young Blood"
- "Searchin'"
- "Yakety Yak"
- "Charlie Brown"
- "Along Came Jones"
- "Poison Ivy"

CHAPTER TWO

Hannah and the Bowling Alley Beast

January, 1958

"This is definitely cool," Tucker yelled over the trumpets from Herb Alpert's Tijuana Brass blaring from the jukebox. No matter where he looked, the gymnasium dance floor was writhing with kids. Others, he noticed, hugged the matted walls and stayed in the shadows.

Tucker's parents had surprised him by permitting him to go to his first Saturday Night Canteen, a weekly dance sponsored by the Police Athletic League.

"Yeah man, it sure is," Kerry agreed, slowly panning the room. "Hey Tuck, there's Hannah *Wart*-finkel. She's in for a long night," he laughed.

Hannah Warfinkel was as plump as Tucker was with a moon shaped face and perpetual sleepy eyes. She wore scuffed brown shoes with yellow socks, and her dress was drab to the point of appearing dirty, despite the lace collar circling her neckline. A cloth stocking cap covered the top of her shaved head, the result of an illness.

Hannah stood alone near the back wall, head bowed, her hands folded in front of her. No boy had asked her to dance, and all rebuffed her requests during "ladies choice."

"What a skeeve," Kerry added.

Tucker looked at his best friend, and then back at Hannah. He remembered what happened to him earlier in the day...

* * *

Tucker reached into the back of the car and pushed aside the heavy sample cases that laid strewn about the floor. They had vaulted off the rear seat when his Dad slammed on the brakes to avoid hitting a kid in the bowling alley parking lot. They now lay in a jumble before him.

Underneath the pile were his new Christmas presents— a pair of bowling shoes, with a matching leather glove and bowling bag. Inside the bag was the best present of all—a new bowling ball. A 14-pound, glossy, black ball with the initials "T.P." stamped onto it. It was a beauty, Tucker thought.

The pudgy 12 year-old grunted, as he hauled the bowling bag over the seat. "Ok. Well, this is it, Dad," Tucker sighed. "It's put up or shut up time."

"Do or die, son," Farmer grinned, hugging him. It was the league championship finals and his son's bowling team was the defending champions.

"Fish or cut bait ..." Tucker muttered. He climbed out of the car, dragging the bag after him.

"Good luck, buddy. Give 'em heck!" Farmer yelled as Tucker slammed the car door closed. "I'll pick you up at noon." Farmer smiled and waited until his son vanished into the bowling alley before easing away.

Tucker unbuttoned his coat and quickly scanned the list

of the team's lane assignments. They were tacked to the corkboard, on the wall next to the men's room. "Please, please," he whispered, and silently prayed that God, in His benevolence, would see to it that his team bowled on lanes 32 and 33. He bowled his best all season long on those two lanes, and God knew it. Besides, he was an Altar Boy and that should count for something.

"Tempor Tool and Dye ... Down Towne Cleaners ... Tupcek Welding ... Tuscanini Dairies. Here it is," he mouthed, running his fingers across the chart. It stopped on lane assignments 32 and 33. "Yessir!" "Alright!" he shouted and half ran, half stumbled past the snack bar, toward the lanes. Over the din of conversation, the low rumble of the heavy balls rushing down the alleys was followed by the sudden, violent explosion of wooden pins.

This was an important day for Tucker. His team was in the championship "Bowl Offs," he had a brand new ball with matching accessories, and tonight he was finally being allowed to go to the Saturday Night Canteen.

So far, the morning was going good except for the news his father greeted him with at breakfast, about Roy Campanella. It was bad enough that the Dodgers abandoned Brooklyn for Los Angeles. This morning their greatest catcher ever, broke his neck in an auto accident. "Campy" Campanella was permanently paralyzed. There just wasn't any justice.

"What a lousy thing to happen," a dejected Tucker sighed. Despite the anger he felt for the Dodgers, he silently dedicated the league Bowl Offs to Roy.

Tucker finished lacing his shoes then stood and straightened his bowling shirt. "Tuscanini Dairies—milk from the old country," was embroidered in red on the back of Tucker's white bowling shirt. Neatly scripted across the left pocket was "Tuck." The leather, fingerless bowling glove molded to a snug *fit on his right hand. He looked good, felt powerful, and believed that nothing could turn his luck today.*

That was until teammate, Carl Maglia, began his approach for a practice roll on lane 32.

Tucker watched as his lanky friend brought the ball to its highest peak, and then began the smooth glide on his left foot. Carl let the ball fall in a natural, gentle, downward arc and readied to release it when his shoe hit a wet spot on the approach lane.

His foot jolted to a halt, while the rest of his body, propelled by the bowling ball, lurched forward. Maglia crashed to the alleyway, directly over the gutter lane, and landed on top of his left forearm. The popping and snapping sounds of bones echoed off the acoustic tiles.

Tucker stood frozen to the floor, aghast, as the team's best bowler stood up. Maglia's left forearm reconfigured into a u-shape, and he was supporting the bottom of it with his right palm.

It was at this point, Tucker would recall later, that things got out of control.

His team was blown out of the first two championship games by Bartolutti's Mortuary; he split the seam in the back of his pants during the second game (ironically, his personal best score of 186); and he was forced to wrap his coat around his waist. It made him feel like he was wearing a diaper, like Baby Huey.

If that wasn't enough, between the second and third matches, Tucker scampered toward the snack bar and accidentally collided with a large, teenage girl spilling soda all over her black leather jacket and red, mohair sweater.

'Why don'cha watch where your goin,' you little porker!" she screamed, while Tucker frantically dabbed at the front of her sweater.

"I-I'm sorry," *Tucker sputtered.* "It was an accident. Here, let me help." He wiped the soda with his hands.

"Get away from me you fat little creep!" the girl shouted, snapping her chewing gum.

"Hey, I said it was an accident and I'm sorry," Tucker replied, his voice rising. "And if I'm a fat little creep, you are a hairy-chested hormone who needs a shave!"

Before Tucker could blink, she yanked him upside down and held him tightly under her arm.

"Let me go!" a squirming Tucker screamed.

The girl stormed over to a trashcan, lifted the lid, and dumped Tucker in upside down. All that anyone could see were two legs sticking up out of the can, kicking wildly, while muffled yells bounced around the bottom.

After a brief struggle, Tucker managed to tilt the smelly receptacle over and crawl out. As he brushed French fries off the sleeve of his bowling shirt, he realized that a crowd of people stared at him.

"What a loser!" one pimply faced kid shouted.

"Gettin' beat up by a girl!" another stranger taunted. The entire crowd erupted into laughter.

Tucker stood paralyzed in the center of the faded carpet surrounded by his friends and strangers. He hated the way the taunting made him feel, and he wanted to disappear. There was no way out ...

"You know what Kerry," Tucker yelled at his friend, "sometimes you're a real jerk." He spun around and elbowed his way through the throng. After feigning and pirouetting through the maze of entwined dancers, Tucker reached the clearing on the other side of the gym. Hannah stood directly in front of him.

"Hi Hannah," Tucker yelled over the music, straightening his tie.

"Hi Tucker," she replied, avoiding his eyes.

"Some dance, huh?" Tucker took a step closer.

"Uh huh."

"I was wondering if you'd ..." Tucker yelled, his words muffled by the music.

"What did you say, Tucker?" Hannah yelled back.

"I said ...," Tucker moved closer, raising his voice, "would you like ..."

"What?" she yelled.

Tucker shouted, "Do you want to dance, Hannah?" at the exact instant the music ended. A hundred pair of eyes swiveled and bore into them. He hesitated, breathed deeply and then grabbed her hands. "Would you like to dance, Hannah?"

Another 45 record plopped on the turntable, and a thudding piano introduced the new song. In the background, Arlene Smith, and the Chantels sang "Maybe."

"Sure," she shouted. "I'd like that."

Tucker led her to the dance floor and held her awkwardly. After stumbling a few times, they settled down and began to dance in sync.

"You sure smell nice, Hannah," Tucker sniffed.

Hannah didn't respond. She looked intently into Tucker's eyes, and then she rested her head on his shoulder.

Profile: Arlene Smith—the Chantels
Interview: September 19, 1989

How did your life change when The Chantels became famous?

"I'm a lonely woman today. That's strange to say. I'm very grateful for everything. It's given me an opportunity to live a special lifestyle. I've been to school in chauffeured driven limousines. I've graduated from professional children's school, which I never would have gone to. I went to Juilliard, and graduated from City College of New York. I maintained my regular stuff, but there's also a little sprinkling of that extra business on the side, which is nice.

"What I regret about it is it does sort of isolate you from everyone else. It's a precarious position. Either you are going to be a 'star' and be totally alienated from society, and enjoy all that goes with it, or you're going to be kind of normal, and non-descript and have your own circle of friends.

"I think that when you straddle both worlds, sometimes it gets a little funny. It gets a little crazy to handle. People assume that you're one way, and if you're natural and yourself, well, they don't understand that.

"People have these pre-conceived ideas of what a theatrical person should be, and when you fall short of it, then there's something wrong. She's stuck up. She's this, she's that, but it's not necessarily the truth. That has always been a struggle, because I've always been myself.

"I was always Arlene Smith, daughter of Iola and Ray Smith, and sister to Ray Bernard Smith. I don't know any different.

The music in the early days of Rock 'n Roll seemed more positive in its lyrics and message. Pop music today is defined by its shock value. Any thoughts why, Arlene?

"I know what you're talking about. I'm an Art History buff and the only way that I can get into history is through the art part of it. Art is indicative of the time in which it was created.

"When you want to know what's happened in a society, you just have to look at the art or listen to the music. If you do that, you can see why our music has fallen apart.

"We had a lot of values in the fifties. I'm sure, across the board, that it was a different time. It was calm, although we had segregation.

"People worked, and I talk a lot about this in the act, the land wasn't wasting away, we weren't abusing it. There was a lot more of a spiritual tone. Sometimes it's scary. It's easy to talk from a perspective, as I know it. It was a spiritual time. People weren't really ugly with each other, and the music reflected that.

"Look at the music videos that you're seeing today, and then look at the breakdown of the laws. When did you ever see somebody walk around naked on the stage? I'm not prudish, but you've got to have some reservation.

"The music now, listen to the lyrics. I don't think we need to sing about suicide, and sing about drugs. There are children coming into my class who are third graders—and some of the rap songs are bizarre—who

> To Doug
> merry Christmas
> and Happy new year!
> Arlene Smith
> 12-99

Arlene Smith
Original Lead Singer & Founder Of The Chantels

can repeat the most intricate, adult message, but you can't get them to memorize something else. It's kind of scary."

What kind of material would you record today?
   "You would have to revamp the message of the songs. The message couldn't be purely sexual or

sensual. It would have to start getting into more spirituality because people, I think, need that in their lives now.

"You watch these Christian stations. They're popping up with some wonderful stuff. People are going to circle around to that. I don't mean to knock today's music. I can't say yes to it. It's not my upbringing. I really think they've gone a little too far.

"I think that people who are in a position to be heard on the radio and be seen on television, pretty much have a moral obligation to the young people, especially in light of the fact that they're in so much trouble."

Do you have to consider what messages you're sending to the audience?

"It's very hard to isolate yourself from just being purely entertaining. These people won't let you do that. There will always be speculation as to what kind of individual you are. People will always set an entertainer up on a pedestal because they're doing something they can't do. So that's problem number one.

"People like to talk about entertainers. They buy up all the gossip magazines. I think entertainers have to be true to themselves and realize that people are looking to them. The market wasn't as young when we were coming through. We were young people singing to older markets. Now you've got older people singing to a younger market. So, of course, you've got to be mindful.

"You see, I'm a black woman who's real conscious of what's going on with some of these young people. You've got 10, 11 and 12 year-olds getting pregnant.

"When Madonna came out with "Like a Virgin," you had little kids singing that song and they may not even know what the words mean. Maybe they don't have anybody at home to explain it. I don't know what other songs she can sing, but certainly there are others. I'm not jumping on her, but just using her as a case-in-point.

"I do think that people should be more responsible for the kinds of messages they send out. Its communication what you sing to the audience. What is the thing that you're saying?

"I mean that music is therapeutic. It answers a lot of problems for people. I ran into a therapist about eight or nine years ago. I was doing a show at The Felt Forum and he told me that he played my music for his patients. It was just so nice because all my stuff is about love and praying. So it doesn't give people a hard time.

"I do think that entertainers need to be more aware of what it is they're sending out to the young people that buy their records. Children are impressionable, and if adults honor performers, children revere *them*.

"Those are the fans, and you don't want to send a whole bunch of kids running to the river."

Partial Discography
ARLENE SMITH: THE CHANTELS
    "He's Gone"
    "The Plea"
    "Maybe"
    "Look in My Eyes"

CHAPTER THREE

Timing is Everything

June, 1958

Tucker sagged against the concrete block wall inside the dugout, physically and emotionally exhausted. Sweat trails divided his face into craggy shaped, dirt covered continents. He didn't remember ever feeling this tired or thirsty, and the jar of ice water he brought to the game had emptied by the end of the second inning ("It's pretty close out there, Tuck. This ought to last you," his mother said). Mercifully, one more out and the game would be over. One more out and he would dive head first, mouth opened wide, into an ice cold glass of soda.

Except for the unusual, and suffocating, early June heat, it was pretty much the way he envisioned the playoff game would end—both teams fighting hammer and tong down to the last batter, into the final inning, for the winning run. Only, in Tucker's version, the Indians would beat the Yankees and go on to the Little League Championship game. However, his team was losing by two runs, 4-2, with the bases empty and two outs.

"Batter up!" barked Stanley, the home plate umpire, reaching for the whiskbroom in his jacket pocket. With crisp, precise movements, he bent over and flicked off the dirt that covered home plate.

Teammate Rusty Volkman stepped into the batter's box and took a couple practice swings. No way Rusty gets on base, Tucker thought. He already held the Little League record for striking out Most-Times-In-A-Row.

"A walk's as good as a hit!" a dejected Tucker yelled, knowing the season would soon end with Stanley barking, "Stuh-rike thuh-ree! Yer outta there!" The only good part would be that Tucker wouldn't have to bat again.

He hadn't done much better than Rusty, grounding out weakly in his two previous at-bats. Of more concern to him was that if Rusty got on base, there would only be one more batter between him and …

"Run Rusty" someone screamed, completing his thought.

The stunned Rusty, immersed in uncharted water, stood frozen in place, before remembering that he was supposed to run if he hit the ball. As the pitcher and third baseman converged on the slow roller, the scrawny, baggie-panted Little Leaguer darted towards first base.

"I got it," yelled the pitcher, reaching down for the ball.

"Outta my way, I got it," the third baseman grunted, and in the resulting collision, Rusty stumbled safely across the bag.

"Oh jeez, this can't be happening," Tucker groaned as a sinking feeling began to rise up inside him. After carefully adjusting his protective cup and helmet, he grabbed a bat and headed toward the On Deck Circle.

Teammate Norman "Needles" Liebowitz stood ready at the plate.

In spite of the packed stands, the carnival-like atmosphere, and cheering friends and family, the last thing Tucker needed was the spotlight. How weird this is, he thought. If Needles miraculously gets on base now, I get up to bat with a chance to win the game—or to lose it, and that is what really bothered him. Lately, it seemed that he was on the losing end of life too often—much more than his share.

In a matter of three weeks: his mother caught him in the kitchen pantry feeding tablespoons of vanilla extract to his flu-ridden, younger sister, Blanche. He had told her it was cough syrup; He nearly burned down the church after dropping a lighted candle into the choir stall during a fit of hysterical laughter. Fellow Alter Boy Buck Radcliffe had looked at him cross-eyed and stuck out his false front teeth while they kneeled at the Altar; and he accidentally threw his Aunt Tina's tiny dog, Lollipop ("It's so small, it fits in the palm of your hand," the ad in the comic book read), out of a three story window into the alley. Tucker was amazed they made plaster casts that small for dogs.

Enough was enough already.

"Keep it alive, Needles," a woman yelled from the bleachers as the pitcher threw toward the plate. The young batter swung and missed the ball by a mile.

Good, Needles, good, Tucker thought. Just two more like that and we can all go home. He wanted his team to win, but he did not want the teasing and embarrassment he would have to endure if he batted … and lost the game.

He most definitely did not want to hear any more taunting, especially from the psycho catcher currently squatting behind home plate. He had no idea that so many words rhymed with Tucker and Pitts.

Tucker scanned the crowd and instantly recognized his father. It was easy enough. All he had to do was look for the only man in the stands wearing a white shirt and tie. It was his trademark. No matter where he was—at dinner, relaxing in front of the television, hitting ground balls to his son after work until dark, or sitting in wooden bleachers on a humid Saturday morning in June—his father wore a shirt and tie. They waved.

Somebody brought their transistor radio to the game, and a jagged-edged Rock 'n Roll song filtered through the murmuring crowd.

The fans suddenly moaned in unison, and Tucker turned to see Needles getting up off the ground. He'd been hit by a pitch and limped towards first, rubbing his left thigh.

Rusty jogged to second base.

"Ok, Tuck. It's all up to you," his coach yelled from the dugout. "Be a hitter."

Tucker walked toward the plate, his heart thundering. "This is just perfect," he mumbled.

"Everybody move in," the catcher yelled, waving his arms. "No stick, here. Hell, if it ain't Peter Pork Chops," he sneered.

Tucker smoothed out the batter's box with his spikes. "Bite me, Ralphie," he shot back, knowing he would eventually have to pay for that comment.

"Ok, you two, shut yer traps and play ball!" Stanley growled and hunched down behind the thick-necked catcher.

Tucker dug in and settled into his best Mickey Mantle stance. The trouble was that he was facing the quickest lefthander in the league. The kid threw a blazing fastball, and a curve that looked like it dropped off a tabletop. This should be humiliating, he thought.

The first pitch was just a blur to Tucker. "Stuh-rike one!" Stanley barked and turned, thrusting his right arm upwards.

"Two more," Ralphie yelled, and whipped the ball back to his pitcher. "I told you he's no batter. He's a pork chop."

The next pitch was outside. At least Tucker thought it was, until the ball slammed on its brakes and made a sharp right turn over the heart of the plate. By the time he swung and missed, the pitcher had the ball back in his glove.

"Stee-rike two!" the Bulldog barked.

"Hang in there, son," Tucker heard his father's voice.

"I'm hanging, alright," Tucker, sighed. Well, this was it. One more pitch and it would be over. He called, "Time out," and stepped out of the batter's box.

"Time out," Stanley yelled, and walked over to Tucker. "Look kid, relax," he said, putting his ham-like arm around Tucker's shoulder.

Tucker stepped back into the batter's box, wiping at the sweat that stung his eyes. He braced himself as the lanky southpaw pitcher wound up and uncoiled, firing a rocket toward home plate.

Tucker remembered the advice that his father gave about timing a pitch, and as soon as the ball left pitcher's hand, he swung mightily.

He didn't know what had felt better—the solid feeling of bat meeting that fast ball just above the trademark, or his recent interest in reading *National Geographic* by flashlight, under his covers.

The crowd erupted, jolting Tucker as he watched the ball sail into deep right field. As he rounded first, the ball skipped between the outfielders and rolled all the way to the fence.

Rounding second, the chubby batter looked over to his third base coach who was frantically waving his arm for him to keep running. Tucker looked back over his shoulder in time to see the ball skid off the base of the wall, eluding the frantic outfielders.

Rusty crossed home plate; Needles scored quickly behind him. Tie score.

Tucker rumbled around third and chugged towards home plate. Out of the corner of his right eye, he saw a figure jump out of the stands and race towards the playing field.

Ralphie Amato straddled home plate in a wide stance and threw off his mask. "Throw the ball, he's comin' home!" the catcher screamed to the second baseman, who took the cutoff throw from the right fielder. He whipped around and fired the ball toward the plate.

Tucker thought that he should slide head first, under the catcher's tag. The ball was definitely going to beat him to the plate, and Ralphie was definitely going to beat him to a pulp.

Instead, Tucker bulldozed into the crouching catcher, like Alan Ameche plunging through the New York Football Giants defensive line.

"Uuughn," Ralphie yelped, flying backwards into the wire batting cage. His eyeglasses flew off his face, and the baseball squirted out of his catcher's mitt.

"Safe!" Stanley screamed.

Tucker jumped on home plate, his arms raised in triumph. His teammates erupted from the dugout and swarmed around him.

"Safe!" Stanley yelled again.

Tucker, confused, looked back towards Home Plate. A wall of red dust swirled around Stanley.

"We won! You did it, Tuck," Farmer yelled, dusting off his shirt and trousers.

Consumed by the excitement, Tucker's Dad raced out of the stands as his son rounded third base, vaulted the fence, and sprinted down the base path behind him.

"The next thing I knew," Farmer panted, "I was swallowing dirt.

While pandemonium rocked the stands, Tucker and his father strolled towards a gleaming, new, yellow, Plymouth Belvedere convertible, with hounds tooth interior, and a date with a couple of ice cold Cokes.

As they pulled away, a fan turned the volume up full blast on his transistor radio, and the shrill, boisterous wail of a saxophone punctuated the revelry. A few staccato notes later, in unison, the home team crowd yelled, "Tequila!"

Profile: Chuck Rio—the Champs
Interview: August 25, 1989

Who wrote "Tequila?"

"I wrote 'Tequila.' It was a little riff that we had for intermission. What happened was we really didn't have a title to it. We knew that we wanted to call it "Tequila," but we were afraid in those days. Our guitar player said to me, 'Why don't you call it Tequila; you drink it all the time.' They laughed and, to me, whenever somebody laughed about something I knew that was a little gimmick.

"But we were afraid that the people wouldn't let the kids buy the record. Back in the 50s, it was like somebody today selling crack. We thought that the parents wouldn't let the kids buy the record if it had anything to do with alcohol.

"Then we thought that we'd spell it differently. Te-ki-la. Then we decided, no, maybe the tequila people would give us some problems. But we decided to do it anyway, and leave the thing open. I went back and put the word "Tequila" later on, and we decided to take a chance with it"

Why aren't there more instrumental hits in Rock music?

"Instrumentals are hard to sell because with vocals, kids sing along with them. Everybody always likes the vocals because you get a chance to sing along. But when you listen to an instrumental, it doesn't give you much to do. If you get something with a good dance beat, you got a chance to do something."

32   *Douglas Forde Simms*

Chuck "TEQUILA" Rio and "THE CHAMPS"

(handwritten inscription: *'89 Brother Doug from the Champs "Tequila" Chuck Rio*)

How did "Tequila," aka "The Big Shoe Dance," get chosen for Pee Wee Herman's movie, "Pee Wee's Big Adventure?"

"Well, the only thing that I can say is Danny Altman probably liked that song and connected it with Pee Wee. Danny did the charts for it. I've worked with Oingo Boingo, and I talked to Johnny, their bass player.

But I never got the chance to thank Danny, myself, personally. But I think that he's the one responsible for connecting Pee Wee with the song.

"I talked with their office, and they'd ask me if what they did helped us any? And I told them a lot. We were getting calls that we'd probably never gotten."

Chuck, what's your impression of contemporary Rock 'n Roll?

"I think it's the only thing to do! I advise anybody to get into the music business. It's been so good to me, and it's all I've ever done in my life. Since I was a kid, all I've ever done is play music.

"I've played instruments from guitar, to piano, to bass, to drums, to sax. I play them all. It's been very, very good to me."

Partial Discography
CHUCK RIO: THE CHAMPS
"El Rancho Rock"
"I'll Be There"
"Tequila"
"Train to Nowhere"
"Midnighter"

CHAPTER FOUR

The Peg Leg Man

November, 1958

1.

The late afternoon sun squeezed through the dusty, metal Venetian blinds, casting bars of shadows throughout the still living room. It bathed the room in a glow reminiscent of the yellow cellophane that covered the showroom windows at Doris's Fabric Corral downtown. Tucker Momentarily regarded the dust particles that danced and swirled in the fading slices of light, then returned to the composition notebook on his lap, writing furiously in his journal.

The words flowed from his heart, to his hand, and onto the spiral bound page. The writing helped to diffuse the awful numbness and confusion. He had never been to a "viewing," as his mother called it, and seeing his Grandpa lying on the satin pillow, his green suit and plaid vest neatly pressed nearly made him faint, but only he knew that. "Get up, Grandpa," he had sobbed last night at the casket, running his finger down the waxy hand of his Grandfather.

In addition, no matter what he did, he could not get the sickeningly sweet smell of the flowers out of his nose.

Tucker sat Indian-style on the floor, leaning against the sofa. Although it was a frigid November day, he wore plaid Bermuda shorts and a white, sleeveless, tee shirt. Both were drenched in sweat. His high pompadour, always so deliberately shaped, lay plastered against his forehead. Sharp, escalating pains increased in his stomach.

"Tuck, are you alright, honey?" Vienna asked. She had entered quietly, setting a tray of cookies, milk, and a peanut butter and jelly sandwich on the coffee table in front of Tucker.

"Uh huh," he nodded, not looking up. He was not all right, but did not have the energy to say more.

Vienna studied her son, and then walked to the Admiral TV hulking in the corner. "American Bandstand is on, Tuck. That'll raise your spirits," she said, turning on the television.

The room suddenly darkened as an advancing thunderstorm erased what was left of the sun. A low rumble of distant thunder accompanied it. Vienna turned on the pole lamp next to the TV and exited as silently as she came in.

As Dick Clark introduced The Bobbettes, the pain stabbed Tucker in his abdomen, nearly doubling him over. "Hunger pains," he moaned, grabbing half the peanut butter and jelly sandwich. He stuffed it in his mouth, and washed it down with several long gulps of the milk. Instead of easing the discomfort, a wave of nausea began to build deep inside his stomach. Tucker tried to concentrate on the music, hoping it would take his mind off the fire in his body.

One, two, three,
Look at Mister Lee,
Three, four, five,
Look at him jive ..."

An ear-splitting clap of thunder followed a brilliant flash of lightening. His mother's collection of rare plates trembled inside the grooved rail that encircled the dining room high above the floor. The heat is so insistent, Tucker thought.

He blinked twice and swallowed hard, the bile threatening to erupt at any time. He suddenly understood that whatever was wrong with him had nothing to do with hunger, and he felt the stirring of fear. The room began to shift in and out of focus, and he could not understand why the Bobbettes were yelling at each other, when they knew how sick he was.

I met my sweetie,
(waddy, waddy, wah)
His name is Mister Lee,
(waddy, waddy, wah) ...

Just as Tucker realized that the raised voices were not coming from the TV at all, the swinging door that divided the kitchen from the dining and living room slammed open. His father backlit by the kitchen ceiling light, stood *(loomed?)* framed in the doorway.

Wordlessly, Tucker's father stormed into the living room and stood directly in front of the hourglass-shaped coffee table his son made for him in Mr. Herbert's Woodshop I class. It had been his Father's Day gift.

"Is this how you mourn?" he droned, leaning on the table with both hands.

Tucker flinched at the sight and smell of his father. The laughing blue eyes were now red, swollen, and watery. His impeccable wavy brown hair was sticking out at awkward angles, and his shirt and tie were uncharacteristically askew. Worst of all was the smell of alcohol.

Without waiting for a reply, Tucker's father turned and walked in front of the TV.

"You are not to listen to this crap!" he screamed, and kicked the TV screen as hard as he could. Tiny shards of glass flew in all directions.

Tucker gasped, violently wretched, and then he was swallowed by the darkness.

> *He's the handsomest sweetie,*
> *(waddy, waddy, wah)*
> *That you ever did see,*
> *(waddy, waddy, wah)*

2.

Farmer stared out of the Surgery Ward Waiting Room window, took a deep pull on the Camel, and exhaled a stream of blue smoke. Raindrops fell in rivulets down the windowpane, bouncing back and forth until they wiped out against the bottom frame. The soft wash of rain against the glass, and the rumble of distant thunder deepened his feelings of dread and guilt. He ran his hand through his hair. It felt dirty.

Time had lost all meaning. He had not slept much since his father passed away. The Memorial Service seemed like it was a month ago. Was it only this morning? Yesterday morning?

He had on the same badly wrinkled suit, and his eyes were streaked crimson from drinking too many beers after leaving the funeral parlor. It was tough enough burying his father, but to have Tucker in emergency surgery on the very same day (*night?*) was just too much to handle. Especially since, he felt responsible for his son's collapse.

He turned and panned the room. It was empty except for Vienna. The faded, green walls were decorated with Woolworth's 5&10 pictures of green, rolling hills, and galloping horses. The worn carpet reeked of stale cigarettes, and the air was thick with the smell of ether.

In one corner, the paint peeled down from the ceiling in a long curly-cue. A circular clock, rimmed in brown, hung over the glass door. Westclox scrolled across the face. The red second hand swept past the 12, officially announcing Midnight.

Vienna sat on the edge of the threadbare couch, hunched over, still wrapped in the cloth coat that she had hurriedly thrown on over her housedress. She buried her face in her hands, mostly to hide swollen eyes and runny mascara. She had not uttered a sound in ten minutes.

He did not know what to say to his wife to make her feel better. What could he say? He knew he had already said too much.

The top half of the waiting room wall was lined with windows that opened onto the pediatric ward. Farmer looked across the dimly lit hall, into the window of a dark room. A night light threw long shadows and silhouetted a Negro man and woman. They were peering down into the white, metal crib. Suddenly the woman screamed, "My baby!" and collapsed into the man's arms. A nurse in a starched, white uniform, and pointy cap, bustled into the room and efficiently escorted the man and woman away.

The door to the waiting room swung open. "Mister and Missus Pitts?" the doctor asked, entering the room. He was tall and athletic, with blue compassionate eyes. A green skullcap covered his head, and a cloth facemask was draped on his chest.

"Yes," they both answered.

"I'm Doctor Leeds. Please sit down," he motioned to Farmer. "Your son, Tucker, had a ruptured appendix. His stomach was filled with the most gangrene I have ever seen. His appendix was removed, and he is in his room asleep from the anesthesia."

"Will he be ok, Doctor?" Vienna asked. Farmer put his arm around her.

"He is a very sick young boy, and his body is poisoned severely. I cannot predict how he will recover. We've done all we can, but I would suggest you pray for him."

Vienna gasped.

"Can we see him?" Farmer asked.

"Of course, follow me."

3.

Tucker looked peaceful enough, Farmer thought, despite the oxygen mask covering his face. His skin was pasty, and his well-coiffed hair was akimbo, but he did not look as if he was in any pain.

Vienna walked to the far side of the hospital bed and held Tuckers hand. It felt like it was on fire. "Tuck? Honey? Can you hear me?"

"Tuck? Honey? Can you hear me?" He wanted to scream out, "Yes, Momma. I can hear you," but his mouth would not open. Not that it really mattered now because he was more interested in the hallway he stood in. It stretched endlessly in front of him, narrowing to a door where a soft glow leaked out from all sides.

He wondered, briefly, if he was in the apartment building in Newark where his Aunt Tina lived. Green and black linoleum squares covered the floor, but the awful odor of ripe cabbage and cigars was gone. Doors lined both sides of the hallway.

He felt absolutely nothing; no pain, no heat, no cold, he was not tired, or sad, or frightened. If anything, he was curious, but mostly he was just there.

"Hello, Tucker," the voice said above him. It was soothing, welcoming, and female.

The same starched nurse that ushered the Negro couple from their child's room entered and briskly strode to Tucker's bed. She took his pulse, listened to his breathing, and then violently shook a thermometer before sticking it in his armpit.

"He feels hot," Vienna said, laying the back of her hand against Tucker's forehead.

The nurse did not respond and removed the thermometer. "It's nearly a hundred and five. The antibiotics are not working.

I've got to call the doctor." She ran from the room as Farmer rushed to Vienna.

"I'm so sorry," he began.

Vienna put her finger against his lips. "It's not your fault, Farmer, so stop it. It has been a horrible day for all of us. We need to pray now." She grabbed his hands, and they bowed their heads in silence.

> *She was the most beautiful woman he had ever seen, except for his Mom, of course. Her eyes radiated the same soft glow that edged around the door at the end of the narrow hallway. Her blond hair flowed behind her, disappearing in the billowing white gown that covered her entire body. The fact that she floated on the ceiling held no special meaning for Tucker.*
>
> *"Who are you? Where am I?" He thought the questions rather than speaking them.*
>
> *"Follow me," she replied, and floated down the hallway. Tucker followed.*

The surgeon who performed the emergency appendectomy on Tucker entered the room, followed by two nurses. They wheeled a cart filled with towels and ice cubes. While one nurse wrapped the ice cubes in towels, the other threw back the blanket and began stripping Tucker of his pajamas.

Farmer and Vienna backed away from the bed feeling numb. Their world was crumbling and spinning out of control. They watched the nurses place the ice packs over Tucker's entire body, while the doctor tried, unsuccessfully, to arouse him.

"He's in a coma," he whispered.

> *"Are you an Angel?" he thought. But she did not answer. Every few feet she turned, looked down at him and smiled, but she remained silent, instead, floating effortlessly towards the luminous door at the end of the hallway.*

Tucker lost count of the number of doors he passed on both sides. They were nothing special. In fact, he thought they were the apartment doors in his aunt's apartment building. Some were slightly ajar, eyes peeking out from behind them. Others needed paint.

However, he did casually note that the closer they got to the door at the end of the hallway, the more ornate the doors became. The wood was lustrous, the handles polished, and each was embedded with stained glass panels.

"Hurry, Tucker," the woman in white urged, floating in front of the glowing door. She turned the handle and pulled it open. The light spilled into the hallway and covered him.

It felt better than anything he had ever felt in his entire life. If it felt like this standing outside the door, he could not imagine what it felt like inside, and he hurried towards it.

Farmer clutched his wife, still not totally comprehending what was happening. In the hospital bed not three feet from them, they watched their only son slip further away, despite the frantic efforts of the doctor and nurses.

"His breathing is erratic and shallow, blood pressure falling," the nurse called out in a detached tone. "He could go into cardiac arrest."

Vienna stood frozen in time, barely breathing herself, and squeezed Farmer's hand until it hurt. "Please, God," she sobbed. "Heal him. In Your Son's name, I pray."

Tucker smiled at the woman and took the final step towards the door. The light was brighter, more intense than a million suns, he thought. There was no heat—just the serenity of well being. As he went to step across the threshold, a hand clamped hard around his left arm and pulled him, instead, through the last door on the left.

"Not yet, Tucker," said the man in the green suit and tan, plaid vest. His blue eyes sparkled.

Tucker stared at the man, who wore a matching green felt snap-brim hat, and stood on one wooden leg. It was the same kind of peg leg Grandpa...

"You're alive," he mumbled, but not low enough that Farmer and Vienna did not hear it.

"He's awake!" Vienna pushed past the nurses. "What did you say, honey?" she gasped, stroking Tucker's head. "Who's alive?"

"The peg leg man," he mumbled. "He stopped me."

"Do you know who the peg leg man is?" the doctor asked Farmer, listening to Tucker's chest.

"His temperature is decreasing, Doctor," the nurse said.

"No, not exactly. My father passed away yesterday, and he wore a wooden leg, but I don't know what Tucker means. Will he be ok?"

The doctor smiled and nodded.

"Go home and take a bath, and get some sleep, Farmer," Vienna said. "I'll stay with Tuck until you come back. He'll be OK now."

The sun poked its fiery edge over the horizon as Farmer got in the Plymouth Belvedere and lowered the convertible top. The sky slowly revealed a glorious morning.

He started the car and turned on the radio. Johnny Maestro's thunderous voice jumped from the speakers.

The angels listened in,
When they heard me praying...

Farmer turned the volume up as loud as it would go, crossed his arms over the steering wheel, and rested his head. At first, the tears filled up in his eyes; then they spilled over his lashes and bounced down his thick beard stubble.

Profile: Johnny Maestro—the Crests
Interview: January 29, 1999

Your stages, for the most part, were street corners in Brooklyn.

"Street corners and whenever we could find some kind of dance, neighborhood dance, we would go and sing. Not professionally; we would never get paid."

When did you know that the Crests were going to be an impact on the music scene?

"Well, I guess, you could say from our first national record which was "16 Candles." At that point we started traveling around the country and seeing the effects of our songs. Quite a thrill."

How did your parents relate to this business?

"As far as my parents go, I never really sat down with them and told them what I was doing. This was done more as fun. I did not consider it seriously, just doing it for the fun of it. I never told them about that until we were ready to sign a contract. I came into the house with a contract and said 'Hey, Mom, Dad, I want you to look at this. The guys and I have signed a recording contract.' At that point they did not even know I was singing. They said 'What is this? A recording contract?'

"So they were very happy about it, even though I had not told them before; but they were happy about it and said I hope you know what you are doing. We signed the contract. Never went to a lawyer. Living on the Lower East Side, my parents never had the need to use lawyers for anything. So we had no idea we needed to go to a lawyer. So I just signed the contract."

How did life change for you as a result of Sixteen Candles?

"The only thing that "Sixteen Candles" did for me was to introduce me to the rest of the country. As I said earlier, financially it really hadn't done anything for us. Our style of living did not change at all. After coming back off the road, we all went back home our parents' apartments on the Lower East Side and continued our lives."

Were you paid for your live performances?
"Yes, but that did not amount to very much. To give you an example, one of the tours that we did at our peak was only earning us, maybe, three hundred and change, a week. That tells you what these people were paying you to perform."

With little or no royalties?
"Exactly. We would go on tours sometimes three months at a time. Of course, we would spend a lot of that money on the road. How far can you stretch $300-$400?"

Which were some of the most unique experiences you ever had?
"I would imagine that first unique experience for me was performing in New York at the Lowe's State Theater, with the Alan Freed Show, the Alan Freed Rock n' Roll Christmas Show, I believe it was. Rubbing shoulders with all the people that I was brought up listening to, sort of like superstars, I guess. Again, here we were with the Harvey and the MoonGlows, the Flamingos, and the Everly Brothers.

"These people were musical gods to me, and here I was backstage sharing dressing rooms, sharing stories, and everything with these guys. And then being on stage and performing in front of thousands of people. This was before we started going on the road. This was our first big performance. It was frightening, very frightening."

What do you think of today's nostalgia, with the rebirth of the '50s-'60s music?

"I think it is, of course, terrific for me. It has kept me working now for many, many years. But to see the people that we were singing to back then now come to shows bringing their children, and their grandchildren and enjoying it equally as well, and learning it as a new music to them is not nostalgia.

"I guess the reason for it now is that it was basic, and it is the root of what the music is today, in the rawest form. I guess the rawness of it is something that is attractive to the ear. Most of these people who are listening to Rock 'n Roll and hear this kind of music, say this is what we are listening to now. It is a lot more pure, you know. The baby's first steps are always the ones you remember."

Martha Reeves (the Vandellas) said that as long as there are Oldies stations, she is as current as any top forty. Do you feel the same way?

"That's right. At this point, there are as many Oldies stations in each major city as there is Top-40. And because of that, we are current.

"People who are into our music, generally love our music. Then again, it does take up a certain area of the music field. They are using '50s and '60s music for commercials, etc. We have our little section. I shouldn't say little. It's bigger than little right now. But there will always be new music and there will always be room for us in there somewhere."

Do you feel any different today than you did when you were singing to 16-year old girls?

"No, as a matter of fact. Age never comes into the

picture whenever I am performing or singing. I feel like I did the day that the Crests and I started. Every time I sing a song, it feels like the first time."

Partial Discography
JOHNNY MAESTRO: THE CRESTS and
THE BROOKLYN BRIDGE
  "16 CANDLES"
  "The Angels Listened In"
  "Step by Step"
  "Trouble in Paradise"
  "The Worst That Could Happen"

CHAPTER FIVE

"Not in your lifetime, pork-o"

September, 1959

1.

"Come on, Blanche! You have been in there long enough," Tucker whined, pounding on the bathroom door. "All the time in the world won't get you ready."

"Shut up, Tucker. That's not nice." Blanche's eight-year old voice sounded muffled behind the wooden door; Billy Boy's incessant quacking from the bathtub added to the cacophony. "At least I don't have fat cooties like you."

"Mom, will you tell her it's my turn to get ready?"

"Stop it this instant, you two!" Vienna yelled from the kitchen. "It's only 6:00 a.m., and I am not ready for your loud mouths. Get out of that bathroom Blanche, now. Breakfast is nearly ready. One more thing—shut that duck up before I shut it up."

The entire house smelled like bacon and fresh-perked coffee. Farmer fried the eggs, over-easy, careful not to splatter grease on his white shirt and tie. Blanche toasted the bread and set the table, while Vienna, dressed in her early morning uniform of leather mules and terrycloth housecoat, padded around the kitchen table, spooning out homemade hash browns, and pouring coffee.

When they sat down, Farmer blessed the meal and then retreated behind the morning newspaper. "Good morning, Breakfast Clubbers." Don McNeil's voice floated out of the kitchen radio's puny speaker. The day was now officially in motion.

Tucker shoveled the eggs into his mouth between bites of rye toast, crisp bacon, and gulps of chocolate milk. His hair poked up from the sides of his head in tousled clumps, his cheeks puffed out, and he chewed his food vigorously.

"Hey, Tucker, you look like one of the Chipmunks," Blanche snickered.

He opened his mouth to speak, instead spitting a wad of toast onto the floor. Dorsey, who sat patiently at his feet waiting for scraps, instantly devoured it.

"Slow down, Tucker, and don't talk with your mouth full. You will choke to death," Vienna commanded. "Where is the fire, for heaven's sake?"

"What's gotten into you lately, Tucker?" Farmer asked, lowering the newspaper. "Yesterday, you were so grief stricken about that plane crash several months ago that killed the Rock 'n Roll people, that you didn't touch your breakfast. What were their names again? Wasn't one called the Big Dipper?"

"That's *Bopper*, Dad. The Big *Bopper*," Tucker sighed.

"Whatever. This morning you are a whirling dervish, rushing around here in a frenzy to get ready for school when every other morning, we have to light a fuse under you. You are eating as if the world is about to end, and last night you rushed me to Robert Hall to buy you new pants, a shirt, and shoes. What's going on?" Farmer asked.

"Nothing is going on, Dad. It is … it is just that I'm not a kid anymore. I am fourteen, a teenager. I am in high school now, and I need to dress better and have a better attitude about school." Tucker smiled, praying that would satisfy them. He did not want to go into more detail.

"Very well, Tucker. That is admirable. Nevertheless, your mother is correct. Slow it down a notch." Farmer disappeared, again, behind the paper.

"Yef fir," Tucker answered, his mouth crammed with eggs. He took a quick gulp of milk and wiped his mouth with the back of his pajama sleeve. "May I be excused now?"

"Yes, you may," Vienna answered.

Tucker pushed away from the table, dumped his plate and glass into the kitchen sink, and hurried down the hallway to the bathroom. Blanche spooned the last of her cereal into her mouth and excused herself to dress for school.

Vienna refilled their coffee cups, lit two Camel cigarettes and handed one to Farmer.

They read the morning newspaper in near silence, the exceptions being an occasional rustling of a page turning, or Joni James crooning, "There Must be a Way."

"Farmer, did you read this article about these beatniks?"

"Uh huh, just some bunch of freaks."

"Do you know why they are called 'Beat?'?"

"I don't know, Vienna. It has certain flair, I imagine." His tone was dismissive.

"It says that they are 'Hipsters, teenagers, and semi-Bohemians who dress in black and sit around in silence staring into their coffee cup at the coffee house.'" Vienna paused to take a deep drag on the Camel.

"Sitting around in silence is not such a bad idea, especially when one is trying to read the morning paper," Farmer muttered.

"Excuse me?"

"Uh ... nothing, Vienna. They are a bunch of morons who follow another moron in California, who goes around saying things like, 'We Beatniks have no gods. Our gods are old Christmas trees rotting in a vacant lot in July.' No right-minded person takes them seriously."

Vienna sat in silence for a Moment. "Do you think Tucker could ever be attracted to them? The article does say 'teenagers.'"

"Ok, Mom and Dad, I'm ready. How do I look?" Tucker entered the kitchen unnoticed. He stood behind his mother's chair, leaning against the refrigerator; his hands shoved into his pockets, and his right leg crossed his left at the ankle.

He wore a charcoal turtleneck sweater beneath the new, pale pink shirt, which perfectly complimented the sharply creased, black trousers. His new, and fashionable, "Flip Tongue" shoes shined with a high polish; his trademark pompadour was majestic in height and thick with Vaseline.

"Is that your father's Old Spice I smell?" Vienna asked.

Tucker nodded his head and grinned.

For the briefest instant, Vienna thought she would cry. What she did not know was that Farmer, too, felt a tug at his heart. It was like the other times in their children's lives when they reached a new stage. Tucker, the little boy, was gone forever.

"No, Vienna, I don't think we have to worry about Tucker becoming a beatnik."

To Tucker he said, "Come on, son, I'll drive you to school."

2.

The hallway was thick with students, most shuffling to their sixth period class. A few of the juvenile delinquents, "J.D.'s" as they were called by Truant Officers, pinned their gum-snapping, teased-haired girlfriends against a locker and groped them.

"Break it up, and get to your next class!" boomed the voice of Mr. Weiner, the Assistant Principal. He grabbed one of the boys by the shirt and shoved him along.

It was Pep Rally Friday, and the corridor was jammed with

members of the football team, the cheerleaders, and the flag twirlers, especially Winnie Hatfield; a tall, leggy blonde-haired woman whose twirling routine made Tucker hyperventilate.

He threaded his way towards his locker, bouncing off the intentional shoulder bumps of upperclassmen sporting crew cuts and wide necks.

The hallway narrowed into an intersection, with a wide thoroughfare, and he turned left, hugging the wall. Across from him, the door to the Principal's Office suddenly banged opened, rattling the frosted glass windowpane.

"... and if we catch you smoking in the boy's bathroom again, Mr. Marino, your parents will be notified, you will be expelled and go straight to Reform School. Do you ..." Emilio Marino exited the office and slammed the door behind him, cutting off the Principal.

Tucker shuddered and quickened his pace, praying that he had not been spotted by the tall, gaunt Marino who, along with fellow nut bag, Roger Cohen, took perverse pleasure stuffing him into his locker at every opening.

He glanced over his shoulder. Marino turned right, rushed through the double doors marked Exit, and disappeared down the steps leading to the basement. It was the floor where the "shop" classes were located—wood shop, metal shop, auto body and mechanics shop.

Tucker reached his locker, but his hands trembled, and he had trouble putting the key into the lock. It was not because of the near run-in with one of the "gruesome twosome," either. That was a piece of cake compared to what was about to happen.

"You need some help?" Kerry asked, grabbing the key from his friend's hands. He was dressed in a jacket and tie, required attire for the football players.

"Jeez, man, don't sneak up on me like that. I'm nervous enough," Tucker grumbled. "I told you that I'm asking Sandy Kubinek to go steady with me this period. Look what I got."

He stood tiptoed on the locker's raised bottom and reached into the top shelf. He pushed aside his transistor radio and retrieved a white cardboard box.

"I bought this down town, at Woolworth's," Tucker said, withdrawing a silver band encircled with hearts.

"Did you ever go on a date with her?" Kerry asked, examining the ring.

"Nah. She smiles at me all the time, so I figure she likes me. Look at me. I dress like the cool people now, and I should have a girlfriend. Besides, I don't see anybody beating down her door."

"Are you wearing Old Spice?"

Tucker glared at his friend. "Yes, I'm wearing Old Spice! Is that OK with you?"

Kerry shook his head. "Ok, Tuck, good luck. I have to get to class. I'll see you after the Pep Rally."

Tucker closed his locker and then melted back into the center of the crowd. He wasn't tall enough to see over most of the students in front of him, and he was jostled and nudged. He squeezed his hand into his pocket to make sure the handwritten note asking her to be his "steady," and the white box, was still there. They were.

It was time to get to the outside of the pack. Although he could not actually see the door, he knew that his classroom was just up ahead on the left, and he edged his way towards the wall. He hated this part.

He broke out of the crowd, not too disheveled, and ten-feet from Mr. Bello's Geography class. Standing just outside the door was Sandy Kubinek gesturing to three girlfriends. Tucker, his heart beating madly, breathed deep and walked towards her.

She is beautiful, Tucker thought, withdrawing the box and note from his pocket. Beautiful! He stared at her blond hair, pulled back into a ponytail, and then let his eyes stray over the cashmere sweater.

Her curves were far more appealing to look at than the ones

thrown by her dimwit brother, George. He was the best pitcher on the Junior Varsity Baseball Team, and Tucker had always struck out against him. He had no intention of striking out with Sandy, or repeating the disastrous results of his 6th grade date with Mimi Fassbender.

At the Saturday matinee, after repeated attempts to put his arm around her were shrugged off, Tucker went to the candy counter and bought the Industrial-size tub of buttered popcorn. He sat in silence the remainder of the movie, eating handfuls of it until the tub was empty, and the butter dribbled down his chin. It was his last date with Mimi.

The success of his plan to win Sandy required a conversion to "cool" status. Tucker had soaked the note in cologne, which asked her to be his girlfriend, wear his "Friendship" ring around her neck, and to meet him after class so they could announce their plans of the future to all who would listen, especially his friends. She did not stand a chance.

Sandy entered the room before Tucker. He knew that all eyes were on him, the new definition of "cool," as he ambled confidently down the aisle toward his seat. He stopped at Sandy's desk, swallowed hard, and smiled. Then he handed her the box and note, without uttering a sound, and dream-walked to the back of the room.

He watched her read the note and then open the box. His heart beat ferociously, and he was certain it would burst through his chest. Although her back was to him, he could imagine the smile on her face. When the bell rang, Tucker waited a few seconds before leaving the classroom. He wanted to give Sandy time to put the ring on her necklace to surprise him. She stood outside the door, between her girlfriends, and grinned as he approached her.

"Hi Sandy," Tucker said. She was not wearing the ring, but he probably had not given her enough time. "So, you want to hold hands?" He reached for her.

Sandy giggled, looked at her girlfriends, and then at Tucker. "Not in your life time, pork-o." She plopped the white, cardboard box in Tucker's hand, turned, and walked away.

Tucker slinked back to his locker, thankful the day was over. He was surprised that he did not feel worse about being rejected. By the time he finished putting his books away, the humiliation disappeared. At least he was still "cool."

The hands landed heavy on his shoulders and spun him around. Roger Cohen, 300 pounds with a pushed-in face, stood next to the sallow-skinned, acne-scarred Emilio Marino. Both were dressed in black chinos, hobnail boots, and leather, studded jackets. Marino's hair was greased back on the sides, but a clump of curls drooped over his forehead.

Tucker licked his lips and blinked. "Well, what do you know? Abbott and Costello meet James Dean."

The last thing he saw and heard before he was slammed into the back of the locker was Marino screwing up his nose and asking, "Are you wearing Old Spice?"

Roger Cohen slammed the locker door shut so hard that the top shelf heaved the transistor radio onto the floor, between Tucker's legs. The impact turned it on.

In the dark, Tucker listened to Herb Oscar Anderson, his favorite radio Disc Jockey, finish singing the show's theme song, "Hello, again, here's my best to you." Then he introduced the Skyliners singing their hit record, "Since I Don't Have You."

Profile: JIMMY BEAUMONT—the Skyliners
Interview: May 18, 1990

Note:
"The Skyliners" original group: Janet Vogel, Wally Lester, Joe Verscharen, Jack Taylor, Jimmy Beaumont

How did you meet your long-time manager, Joe Rock?
"I met him at a record hop in the Mt. Washington section of Pittsburgh. He was managing another group called the Crescents. He was also the lyricist on 'Since I Don't Have You' and most of our earlier records. I was singing with the Montereys as a bass. I did one lead, and Joe was impressed with what he heard and asked me to join the Crescents. I joined the group and became the lead singer."

How did the Skyliners come to be?
"I knew Joe Verscharen from high school. We both went to Carrick High School in Pittsburgh. Janet Vogel went to a Catholic school in the Carrick area. We knew her from going to dances in the area.

"The Crescents were together from the time I was 15 until I was 17. We had record contracts, but we never got into the studio with them. Some of the guys were getting disgusted and dropped out of the group. Wally Lester was singing top tenor with the Crescents, so he dropped down to second tenor. We took Janet and put her on top. Joe Verscharen stepped into baritone and Jack Taylor, who had been the guitar player with the Crescents, was also a good singer, so he took over the bass part.

Jimmy Beaumont
and
THE SKYLINERS

Since I Don't Have You
This I Swear
It Happened Today
Lonely Way
Pennies From Heaven

How Much
Believe Me
Comes Love
I'd Die
Where Have They Gone

"That's how we formed the Skyliners. We actually still called ourselves the Crescents until we made the record."

Who influenced your vocal style?
"I guess I was six or seven, watching the Ed Sullivan Show. I would see guys like Vic Damone,

Frankie Laine, Eddie Fisher. When Doo Wop surfaced, I heard the Moonglows; Bobby Lester was a big influence, the Platters, Nate Nelson and the Flamingoes."

How was "Since I Don't Have You?" created?
"That was just a few months after Janet and Joe came into the group. Joe was on his way to rehearsal one night, and his girlfriend had just moved away. Joe had been writing songs, and he was jotting down lyrics on the way to rehearsal, and the song started to come together. By the time he got to rehearsal, it was finished. He gave me the song. The next night I came in with the musical composition. We started rehearsing it, and it just fell into place."

How did having a hit record effect the Skyliners?
"At that time, I didn't have time to think about it. We were on the road most of the time. The record broke in Pittsburgh first. Then Alan Freed played it. It didn't take very long for us to start on the road.

"I guess your head swells up a bit until you find out that's not the way to be. There are a lot of experiences that teach you that. You can't help but think you're just a little bit special, when you're that young. I didn't really let it get to me, from what everyone tells me."

You used strings and brass in your recordings. Whose influence was that?
"I remember sitting in the high school auditorium listening to the Platters' "Twilight Time." They had strings on their stuff. We always said that when we do a make a record, we're going to use strings, too, because it adds class.

"Yes, I would have to say that the Platters did

influence us. When we got the chance to get a girl in the group I thought that was just what we were waiting for."

Who did you tour with?
"We toured with the Drifters, the Coasters, Paul Anka, Annette, Duane Eddy, Jackie Wilson, Lloyd Price, Fats Domino, Bobby Darin. We would go out 30 days at a clip. The acts that were headlining would travel in their cars. On the bus tours, Dion (Dion and the Belmonts) and I would sleep on the luggage racks in the bus so we could stretch out a little bit. Pretty soon, everybody was trying to do that."

How were the Skyliners received by audiences?
"We always got a great response. A little shocking was at the Apollo Theater. "Since I Don't Have You" was number one, or just about to be number one, in the R&B category when we went into the Apollo. We had just come from doing the Alan Freed Show, and we pulled up in our station wagon with our name on the door. There would always be a lot of people backstage at the Apollo on Monday, when the new acts would start the week. They wanted autographs.

"When we pulled up, they couldn't believe that we were a white act because we sounded on the record like a black group.

"I thought this was going to be a tough audience. When we went on the stage for the first time, the people in the audience were pointing and laughing, and it was chaotic. Then it got quiet, and I thought, man, it's time for me to do something. We'd better be good. So, coming to the end of the song, it was still very quiet. When I started to sing the 'you, you,' a lot of the guys in the audience started to sing it with me. Then Janet sang her soprano part, and the women started to sing her part. By the time the song was over, the place was in bedlam, and they all stood up screaming and hollering. What a great thrill. It was something to remember."

Who are today's Skyliners?
"Rick Morris, Donna Groom, and Bob Sholes are with me on Classic Artists Records."

You have two daughters. Would you advise them to go into show business?

"That's tough, because the younger one is thinking about that. I just told her that it's a tough business and to think twice. Get ready to have your heart broken a lot of times."

Partial Discography
JIMMY BEAUMONT: THE SKYLINERS
"Pennies From Heaven"
"Since I Don't Have You"
"This I Swear"
"Three Coins in the Fountain"
"Lonely Way"

CHAPTER SIX

When You Wish Upon a Star

May, 1960

    The kitchen was quiet except for the low hum from the refrigerator motor, and the "tick, tick, tick" of the Tea Pot wall clock. It struck Tucker odd how a room, which vibrated with so much life and energy in the daylight, could now be so silent and still in the moonlight. It felt like the kitchen was asleep, along with the rest of the house.

    His parents, exhausted from the long drive home, from South Carolina to New Jersey, had gone to bed right after Ed Sullivan. That was good, Tucker thought. He was still burning inside with excitement and could not sleep. A kaleidoscope of images and sounds from the weeklong journey erupted in his mind, and he wanted to wallow in them a while longer. He didn't feel like having any conversations tonight, with anyone.

Tucker leaned against the kitchen counter, lighted only by the orange nightlight plugged into the wall next to the toaster, and started to pour a glass of milk.

"No! Not that glass, Tucker," Vienna snapped, flicking on the ceiling light.

"W-what?" Tucker, startled, spilled milk on the counter. "Jeez, Mom, don't scare me like that. I thought you were asleep. Why can't I use this glass?"

"Because I said so, that's why! Because it is a beer glass, and if you pour milk in it, the taste is ruined. Use a jelly glass. In addition, I have told you a million times not to use the Lord's name in vain. 'Jeez' is disrespectful to Jesus. Understand?"

"Sure. Yeah," Tucker answered.

"Yes," Vienna corrected.

"Yes, what?"

"You answered 'yeah,' when you should have said, 'yes,' as in, 'yes, mother.' Do you understand *that*?"

"Yup," he replied.

"Are you getting fresh?" Vienna stood face-to-chin with her son. "I don't care that you are taller than me now, buddy boy, because I'll smack your face. Finish your milk and get to sleep." She wheeled around, slammed off the kitchen light, and stormed from the room before Tucker had a chance to reply.

He sponged up the spilled milk, replaced the cardboard stopper on the top of the milk bottle, and put it back into the Kelvinator. Then he disappeared into his bedroom and closed the door.

Tucker liked being alone in his bedroom. It was his fortress, and it felt safe. Sometimes, it was magical. Certificates of honor and achievement, of one kind or another, papered the walls. Thumb tacked above a wooden bookcase filled with the entire Hardy Boys collection was a New York Yankees' pennant. Bowling trophies of varying sizes rested on the top shelf. Hundreds of glow-in-the-dark stars, pasted there years ago by his father, transformed the ceiling into his private universe.

He turned on the night lamp that sat on the nightstand between the twin beds. After kicking off his black P.F. Flyers and stretching out on top of the taffeta bedspread, Tucker grabbed the transistor radio, dialed in to WINS, and placed it on the pillow next to him. He wasn't sure which disc jockey was on the station, because Alan Freed had just been arrested for "payola," was fired from his radio and TV shows.

Ah bey,
Ah bey,
Kooma zowah zowah.

Good timing. Murray-the-K was starting another "swinging soiree." It was the signature chant of his show and mimicked in the halls of Tucker's high school.

Tucker clasped his hands behind his head on the pillow and let out an audible sigh. He hated it when he "butted heads," as his grandfather used to say, with his mother. Lately, it seemed that she had begun yelling at him for no reason at all, and it was happening more and more. It was not just the sudden outbursts from his mother that confused him, either. He was going through changes.

Yes, he was being "fresh" to his mother, and he knew it. He didn't mean to be, but he couldn't help it. At those times, he felt like he stood outside his body and watched another Tucker say mean and hurtful things to her.

Since the end of last summer, Tucker had grown nearly three inches, lost twelve pounds, sprouted pimples, and finally discovered his first body hair after months of self-examination. His voice deepened, and he stopped parting his hair and combed it straight back instead. The pompadour was history. Wildroot Creme Oil replaced Vaseline, and Aqua Velva was added to his after-shave repertoire. He had taps put on the heels and toes of his shoes, like the "cool" people.

Tucker felt restless. Surely the fact that it was spring, and that his first year in high school was near an end, had something to do with that, but it went deeper. The high tenor voice coming from the radio diverted his attention.

Sorry, sorry, oh so sorry.
Uh oh. I ran all the way home,
Just to say I'm sorry.

Tucker shuddered. It was the Impala's hit song, "Sorry." Yeah, that's about right, he thought. Sorry pretty much described his school year. Not the academics. He got an "A" in English [his teacher, "Ma" Baker, reminded him of the matronly, stern, but fair Aunt Bea on The Andy Griffith Show and Algebra I. He also received an "A" in gym, although he hated wearing the stupid blue gym shorts, new athletic supporter and white tee-shirt; but it was better than the dumpy one-piece uniforms the girls had to wear.

It all started to go wrong for him last autumn, at the"36th Annual Thanksgiving Football Classic" between Irvington and West Side. While the brand new 7,500-seat bleachers were being dedicated, Tucker, along with new friends Bobby Betts, Jimmy Fellini, and Sheldon Moskowitz, stood huddled beneath the seats.

Betts had a wide, flat face, hooded eyes, and a high forehead that contrasted with his ever-present sidekick, Fellini, who was thin and feral. Moskowitz, a hulking Neanderthal, was a known bully. Ten years later he would be in Sing Sing, on death row, for gunning down Police Officer Robert Oberto, Irvington High School's starting Center in the Thanksgiving Day football game.

"Who's got butts, Betts?" Moskowitz asked.

Fellini howled and slapped Moskowitz's back. Betts pulled a pack of Parliaments from his jacket pocket, and, after lighting one up, passed the pack to Fellini and Moskowitz, who followed suit. Tucker declined.

"What? Are you a toad, man?" Moskowitz sneered.

"Come on, Pitts," Betts urged, blowing a stream of smoke into Tucker's face.

Tucker remembered watching as his cousin, Charley, caught by his father with a cigar, was forced to smoke one after another until he turned green. But these guys were cool, and they did not mind him hanging around with them. He felt like he was one of the "Bowery Boys."

"Give me a drag of yours," he said to Fellini, who handed him the cigarette. Tucker sucked some smoke into his mouth and began choking immediately. "Nah," he gasped, handing back the Parliament. "Who has a stick of Blackjack? I can't have my parents smelling smoke on my breath."

If it had ended there with the smoking experiment, it would have been bad enough. It did not. It got worse. The three of them, on Saturday afternoons, began stealing 45-rpm records from Woolworth's, and they were never caught.

Whenever he wanted money to buy an extra chocolate chip cookie at lunch, Tucker took the change from the weekly church offering envelope.

Emboldened, on a sunny Friday, walking home with Betts and Fellini after school, Tucker accepted their dare and heaved a brick through the windshield of a Chevy sitting on the Jobson's Used Cars lot.

In slow motion, he had watched the red brick tumble, end over end, clear the hanging bare bulbs and colored pennants, and explode through the windshield. Everything screeched to a halt in Tucker's mind—the cars, the street noise, and the wind. Butterflies froze in mid-flutter.

Fellini and Betts shrieked and scattered. Tucker stood transfixed, partly because he was unable to believe what he just did. This was so much worse than when Blanche knocked his mother's antique vase to the floor while practicing new moves with the Hoola Hoop and then blamed him.

He was peripherally aware that his two "friends" had bugged out on him. The only thing to do was run. Instead of running away from the car lot, Tucker ran directly into it, down the center aisle, hoping that the owner would not expect that. He ducked down behind a yellow Nash Rambler, peeked around the bumper, and under the car. The coast was clear.

Tucker turned to run, but blocking the sun, and him, was the largest man he ever saw. A meaty hand, nearly the size of a dinner plate, clamped onto the back of Tucker's neck. The harder he struggled, the harder the giant squeezed, and the worse the pain. Tucker thought he might empty his bladder, or faint, or both.

"You ain't going nowhere, you little punk," the man yelled, dragging Tucker into the small sales office. He shoved him onto a wooden folding chair, next to a TV that had a box of partially eaten, powdered donuts sitting on top of it. Aluminum foil covered the tops of the rabbit ears antenna. The huge man paced back and forth, his face red; a vein throbbed in his neck.

At first, Tucker whimpered, and then he broke into deep, heaving sobs. "I-I'm sorry, mister. I'm so sorry. Oh, my God, what did I do?" He eyes and nose leaked.

"I ought to get the school traffic cop on the corner! You'd go right to the pen. That's where you belong, pally. That's what I *ought* to do."

Tucker moaned. "Oh, sir, please don't. I'll never do this again. I swear to God. Oh please, oh please, oh please."

The man continued pacing, occasionally glancing at Tucker, who had begun to hyperventilate.

"Well, stop bawling and calm down. Eat a donut, and give me your parents' names and phone number. I know who your pals are, and they are trouble. Stay away from them for your own good."

"I-I promise," Tucker sniffed. "Do you have to call my parents? I'll get a job and pay you for the window."

The giant scratched his scalp. "That's sounds fair. Now you get out of here, and I'll think about it. But don't ever do anything like that again, 'cause if I catch you ..." he let the sentence linger for effect. "Well, let's not think about *that*. And take an extra donut with you."

Tucker scribbled down his phone number, bolted through the office door, and ran all the way home. That was two weeks ago, one week before the unexpected trip to Parris Island. The giant man still had not called.

He changed the radio station to WMCA, and the machine-gun delivery of "Jocko" Henderson screamed from the radio.

This is your ace from outer space. Not the duplicator, not the imitator, not the impersonator, but the originator. And here we go, with the hottest show on the radio. Come on now. You can make it on Jocko's Rocket Ship.

The Flamingos began "I Only Have Eyes For You." Tucker loved their songs, their voices, and their harmony. In fact, he loved all the vocal groups, but especially the Black groups. Some of them made him feel as if he was in church, and they were the choir. He understood that there were certain songs and groups that bypassed his eyes and ears and went directly to his soul.

Then last week, his father announced that they were all taking a road trip to see his cousin Donny, Charley's older brother, "graduate from the Marine Corps Boot Camp at a place called Parris Island." It was as if God Himself had planned this trip, Tucker thought. He fingered the brochures next to him on the bed.

On the morning of the graduation ceremony, the sun was a brilliant, lemon-colored yolk suspended against a cloudless South Carolina blue sky. It was uncharacteristically cool for September, but Tucker was glad he was in a short-sleeved shirt. The reviewing stand and bleachers were jammed with proud friends and relatives. Others snapped photos in front of the famous statue of WW II Marines raising the American flag on Iwo Jima.

Tucker watched the graduating platoons pass by, hundreds of new Marines, heads shaved, all in perfect step and guided by intimidating Drill Instructors shouting unintelligible, singsong cadences. The Marine Corps Band played "The Marine's Hymn." It was almost more than Tucker could take. He had never experienced anything like this, and he knew, right then and there, that he wanted to be a part of what Cousin Donny called, "an elite band of warriors."

He was now determined to get into Marine Corps shape. Most of all, Tucker was inspired by the Marine Corps motto, Semper Fidelis, always faithful. He knew without a doubt, that God must have been a Marine.

Tucker, dressed in the official Marine Corps PT gear that his cousin gave him as a gift, slid off his bed and laid face down on the floor. He placed the palms of his hands flat against the hardwood, took a deep breath and pushed up.

"One ..." down slowly, exhale, deep breath.

"Two ..." up.

"Three ..." down.

"Four ..." up.

Profile: TONY CARLUCCI—the Impalas
Interview: October 18, 1989

Note
Original members: Richie Wagner, Tony Carlucci, Lenny Renda, Joe Frazier

How did a neighborhood candy store figure into the Impala's rise to fame?
"Well, there were four or five stores on the block, and the candy store was right on the corner. We used to wait until 9-9:30 at night, when all the stores were closed but the candy store, and we would go into a little hallway to get some kind of echo and be out of the way. We would practice there every night."

How did your life change going from the street corner, singing in a candy store, to having a hit record?
"At first, I didn't know what was going on. I don't think any of us did. I mean everything happened so fast, from the street corner to the stage, from the stage to collecting a Gold Record. It was like you close your eyes, and you wake up, and you're in the middle of a dream. It's an experience everybody should go through.

"You also find out who your buddies are. You find out who sticks by you, who ignores you, and who still talks to you. If you talk to anybody who's made it, and they say nothing changes, then they're fooling themselves."

What are some of your favorite memories of your success with the Impalas?

"We finished a one-nighter in Washington, D.C., and I guess it was just a bad part of Washington where we did it, but by the time we went on, the crowd was getting rowdy. Little Anthony and the Imperials followed us.

THE IMPALAS
CUB RECORDS

GENERAL ARTISTS CORPORATION
NEW YORK   CHICAGO   BEVERLY HILLS   DALLAS   MIAMI BEACH   LONDON

"After the show, we got on the bus, and we were starting to come out of the parking lot when rocks started to hit the windows.

"The bus driver, who was about 6'5" and over 300 pounds, turns and says to everyone, 'Ok, who's coming out?' Well, we were the only ones who got up. The six of us went out there, and there was no trouble at all. We just told the trouble-makers that we didn't come here for any trouble and got back on the bus.

"I understand that Little Anthony had a hard time. Things started to fly, and they had to leave in the middle of their number.

"There was one experience where we were kidnapped. We were signed up to do one show in Allentown, Pennsylvania. We came into the airport, and this lady approached us, with her driver, and said that she was from such-and-such radio station, and that was the radio station that we had to go to.

"Well, we ended up at a high school dance. When my manager approached her about it, she said that it was for publicity. We did our show, and by the time we found out what happened, it was too late to do the radio show. We thought it was a joke until we found out that it had hurt us in a way. We still had to do that radio show.

"Our manager said to give us a check, which they did, and it bounced. You live and learn. We were so green at this it wasn't funny."

Do you feel a connection between the days of Doo Wop and pop music today?

"Not at all. I much prefer to listen to the music from 25-years ago. Not because I grew up in that era, but because the music today is just mind-bending.

"It just makes me think about the good old days, and they were. They were fantastic days. Whether there was money to be made or not, if they told us 'we'll just pay your expenses,' I'd go. It was just that way at that time.

"I'd say that today, the artists, or the record companies, are just going for the money. Back then, I can say for myself, that the money was good, but it was more than that. I remember our first show. I was watching these people out there, watching me entertain them. The people who go to concerts today are stoned to begin with, and maybe they hear the music, and maybe they don't."

Partial Discography
TONY CARLUCCI: THE IMPALAS
"Sorry (I ran all the way home)"

CHAPTER SEVEN

A Siren's Song

August, 1960

Journal entry
Point Pleasant Beach, N.J.
Monday night (2100 military time)
1 Aug 60 (how the Marines write the date)

My head is dizzy—swimming. I want to cry, and I want to throw up, yet I have never felt so alive! But I'm scared, and I think I wet my pants. Not exactly the way I thought my 15th birthday would end.

It started just fine; the way Dad planned it. He woke me up at 0530 (military time) by flipping on the bedroom light and singing "Happy Birthday," but not loud enough to wake Mom or Blanche. Dorsey was lying on the foot of the bed snoring louder than Dad sang. He was still exhausted from running on the beach with me yesterday, and I had to prod him with my foot to wake him up. He just grunted a sleepy woof and rolled over (Dorsey, not Dad).

Anyway, Dad promised to take me fishing for my birthday, and I dressed quickly, eager to get to the inlet by 6:00 a.m. I like that time of morning. It's so peaceful and quiet. There are a handful of cars, but mostly empty streets and flashing yellow lights. I like the wet, salty air, and the oily aroma of the fishing docks, where Arnie Carlson's lobster boat dumps hundreds of pounds of lobster twice daily.

Dad and I, sometimes Mom and Blanche, too, get down to the docks and wait for Mr. Carlson to bring in his old boat, the Sweet Meat. We buy a lot of fresh lobsters, clams, and corn-on-the-cob and host the "Pitts Friday Night Clambake." We set up the long tables, and chairs, and put the lobster pots on the grill. Kegs of beer, lots of friends and family come, and many leave pretty loaded. The best part is the college-girl waitresses from the Lobster Shanty. Man, I love their gold uniforms! They think I don't notice, but I do.

Dad put the convertible top down on the Plymouth, and we crawled north along Ocean Avenue, paralleling the Atlantic. It was humid, despite the early hour. Where the beach meets the jetty, we turned left, alongside the inlet, past the metered parking spaces on the right and parked in our usual spot in front of Carlson's Bait and Tackle. We ate a quick breakfast of pancakes and bacon at the Pink Flamingo Café, next door to the bait shop (a ritual that goes back as far as I can remember, and where Dad and I watched the Andrea Doria sink after colliding with the Stockholm, four years ago, over eggs and bacon), and then we were ready to fish.

We bought squid and bloodworms (ugly suckers), hoping to snag some flounder. This might be a good time to introduce the new cap Dad wore. It was a Christmas gift from me, and he waited all year to wear it on our fishing day. It was a beauty, too. Thin black and red velvet stripes from *front to back. He looked so cool wearing it, especially driving the Plymouth convertible. That's why what comes next is so ... painful.*

The Manasquan Inlet is relatively gentle until it reaches the jetty, where it meets the Atlantic Ocean head on, and then it all goes bad. The waves crash over the jutting rocks, and the commercial fishing boats bounce violently until they reach the ocean.

We set up close to the bait shop, right behind the sea wall. The sky had lightened, but it was still too dark to see where your hook and sinker splashed.

I baited my hook with a fresh slice of squid, long and tapered. Dad used a bloodworm. Once, one of them bit him. It just clamped down on the tip of his finger. They have these grotesque sucker hooks at the end of their body; I think they are from another planet (the bloodworms, not Dad). Well, sometimes I think Dad came from one of those giant pods in "The Invasion of the Body Snatchers."

After first casting his line in the water, Dad stood off to the side, holding a red thermos cup filled with steaming hot coffee in his left hand. In his right, he gripped the fishing pole at the base. He nodded, my signal to cast my line, and then he turned toward the inlet, his back to me.

The truth is that I can cast a fishing line pretty good, but not this time.

I slid the reel lock to off, held the fishing line down against the reel with my thumb, and whipped the fishing pole over my right shoulder. A key to a successful cast is the timing of the release of your thumb on the reel. If you hold it too long, your line can fall short. If you let it go too soon, your line can go wild, which is exactly what I did.

First, I heard the sickening thud of the eight-ounce lead sinker hitting the back of Dad's skull. Frozen in terror, I watched as the hook (the squid dangled like a hanged-man) pierced the base of Dad's neck and slid up the curve of his head, carving out a mini-trench, until it caught on his new cap. The momentum of the sinker rocketed the hook, squid, and Dad's cap, into the middle of the inlet. In seconds, all three slid beneath the waves.

I sighed and turned toward Dad. He was on his knees, holding a handkerchief against the back of his neck, and jerking his fishing pole. I still don't know if he was whipping that pole back and forth because he is just that good a fisherman (which he is), or if he was in shock. The way that sinker hit his head, it's no wonder he didn't completely blow a fuse and short-circuit.

Anyhow, I had just helped him to his feet, apologizing profusely, when something yanked hard, very hard, on Dad's fishing pole. It nearly jerked it right out of his hand. We both completely forgot about the crimson furrow in the back of his neck, instead focusing on the struggle he was having with whatever was on the end of the hook. For certain, it wasn't a flounder.

Dad yelled, with excitement mostly, as the pole nearly snapped in half. The fish on the other end battled fiercely, violently whipping the line back and forth. Through it all, Dad kept pulling up on the pole, and then reeling in the slack. I didn't notice at first; because I was too busy watching him fight this monster, but a small crowd of fishermen gathered in a semi-circle behind us, quiet as church mice.

Twenty minutes later, the eastern sky brightened as the sun snuck its way up towards the horizon. I could see the surface, now, and Dad's fishing line vibrated crazily in the frothy water. There was an audible gasp from the small, but growing, crowd. And then I saw the dorsal fin break the surface. Dad caught a hammerhead shark, about six-feet long.

Like a pro, Dad played the shark, side-to-side, tiring it out, until the will to fight was gone. He pulled it as close to the sea wall as he could, just enough to see the shark's dull, black eyes glare at him, and then he cut the line.

I got chills when the crowd cheered and applauded. We stayed a while longer; each of us caught two sizeable flounder, but after the shark fight, it didn't have the same excitement. We packed up and left. Good thing, too, it started to rain hard ...

Tucker stood up, stretched, and walked barefoot across the planked deck of the back porch and leaned against the decaying wooden rail surrounding it, careful not to get splinters in his feet or elbows. Last week, the first of the family's two-week summer vacation, a two inch jagged shard pierced deep into the ball of his left foot, and it took a trip to the Point Pleasant Hospital Emergency Room to remove it. It wasted five hours of their vacation, and his parents weren't at all happy.

He adjusted his black, linen, Bermuda shorts (a birthday present from Aunt Tina) attempting to free himself from the dampness and stickiness. The air was dead still, not a breeze blowing. The wretched August humidity, even at ten o'clock at night, cloaked Tucker in sweat, although it was not the sole reason for his discomfort. It wasn't any cooler inside, despite the three floor fans pushing the hot air around on High speed. At least they kept the mosquitoes at bay.

The rear of the summer bungalow faced the Atlantic Ocean. The beach stretched north, to the inlet, and south, past the bright lights from the Amusement Park on the boardwalk, eventually disappearing into the night. Clusters of sea gulls, balanced on one leg, dotted the sand, and huddled together for protection. In the blackness beyond the breakers, ships' lights blinked and twinkled as they passed each other in search of a friendly port.

Tucker leaned his head back, closed his eyes, and breathed deeply. The gentle surf washed up on the shore, carrying with it the shrieks of teenagers on the thrill rides. Ordinarily, he would sulk about not being allowed to go to the boardwalk at night without adult supervision, but not tonight.

He walked back to the bench, next to the screen door, and sat down. Bathed only in a solitary porch light, he turned on the transistor radio, picked up his ballpoint pen, his notebook, and continued to write.

> *... The rest of the day went well, if you don't count Uncle Frank nearly setting the bungalow on fire at my birthday party—more on that in a moment. I worked a couple hours at the Fish House bussing tables at lunchtime. Normally, the place was crammed with tourists, but since it was pouring cats and dogs, there were just two customers.*
>
> *I hung out in the kitchen, sipping a Coke, and brushing away the food that was splattered across my apron. Chunks of fish scales, shrimp shells, hush puppies, and Cole slaw hung off me like Christmas tree ornaments. I skeeved it, but it was spending money. What I didn't understand was why June, the 17-year old, shapely, but dumb-as-dirt, lunch-shift waitress, kept grinning at me from across the room.*
>
> *"Happy birthday, Tuck," she said, leaning on the prep table. Then she slowly pulled her uniform's zipper down the front far enough to reveal more than I was expecting. "I have a little present for you."*
>
> *I swear she heard me gulp, and I couldn't help but stare. What broke my trance was when she scrunched up her nose, puckered her lips, and threw me a kiss. I thought I was going to lose my lunch. She wasn't too bad to look at, really, if you could get past the protruding front teeth. But her face was long, and when she smiled, I wanted to throw a saddle on her.*
>
> *"Oh, yeah, what present," I stammered? It was the only thing I could think of. But before she could answer, her customer yelled for more iced tea, and she hurried out of the*

kitchen. I split before she came back. It was time to go home and get ready for my birthday dinner.

It wasn't actually a dinner, just a barbecue with most of my aunts, uncles, and cousins from Dad's side of the family; except the rain forced the barbecue indoors. That wouldn't have been too bad, broiling the hot dogs and hamburgers in the oven, but Uncle Frank insisted (and that was peculiar because he rarely speaks—I should have seen it coming), we bring the barbecue grill into the house and grill on the screened—in front porch.

Uncle Frank is blind in one eye and has no teeth. He doesn't wear an eye patch, and his eyelid gets sucked into the empty eye socket. It's pretty funny. His favorite meal is a soup sandwich.

Why Dad let him be in charge of the grill is a mystery. Maybe his thinking processes were messed up from being hit in the head with that lead sinker.

Anyhow, Uncle Frank emptied an entire bag of barbecue briquettes into the grill and doused them with lighter fluid. I mean he doused those things for about five-minutes. The problem arose when he didn't notice the hole in the bottom of the grill, or the pool of lighter fluid collecting at his feet.

Aunt Tina walked in, smoking a Chesterfield, and ranting about Eleanor Roosevelt and John Kennedy. "Who's this guy, Kennedy, anyway?" she slurred. "A Catholic and a Democrat? God spare us." After a couple of beers, she's something else.

"He's from Camelot, Tina," Uncle Frank said. "I heard Walter Cronkite say so."

She started to reply, but she had sucked in a large lungful of cigarette smoke and started choking. Stuff was coming out of her nose.

"That's in England, ain't it?" he continued. "We beat those limeys fair and square." It was at that moment that he *decided to reenact the Revolutionary War, swinging his arms about as if he was sighting in on the Red Coats. Unfortunately, Aunt Tina's choking convulsions moved her to the right of, his blind side, as he flailed away. His arm hit her wrist, jarring the cigarette loose, and into the puddle of lighter fluid.*

Dad heard the screams of "Fire!" and "Holy crap" and ran in with a vase filled with water. Behind him were Mom, Uncle Bo, Cousin Mikey, and Aunt Corrine, all carrying various containers of water. They quickly doused the fire climbing up Uncle Frank's pants, and soaked the entire grill. So much for hot dogs. We ended up going out to the diner.

After everyone went home, Mom and Dad said they were going out, alone, for a couple hours, and a baby sitter would stay with me. Despite my howls of protest ("I'm 15-years old, Mom!"), there wasn't going to be any negotiation ("You want to live to see 16?").

The knock on the door sounded promptly at 8:00 p.m. I heard Mom speaking to a girl in the doorway; the voice sounded familiar. When she came in, I felt weak. It was June.

Mom and Dad left, and after some uncomfortable chit-chat, June put a stack of 45s on the turntable, and pulled me up off the couch to dance. She didn't say a word; she just yanked me to my feet. Santo & Johnny played "Sleepwalk," and the Hawaiian Steel Guitar relaxed me.

Everything happened so fast. She put her arm around my waist and pulled me into her. I don't know why I didn't stop her. My heart felt like it would explode right through my chest, and I had some trouble catching my breath. Her perfume was powerful, and I found myself sniffing her neck. Then she slid her hand into mine and put her head on my shoulder.

"You look good, Tucker," she whispered into my ear. No girl had ever said that to me before, especially in that tone. I couldn't talk, and my ability to think had long since abandoned me.

We danced in silence, slow, and then she leaned in close and stuck her tongue in my ear. If I had to explain what that felt like, the closest I could come was when I was seven years old; I touched an exposed, frayed electric lamp cord at Kerry's house. Being electrocuted isn't a feeling one is likely ever to forget. The tip of her tongue buried in my ear had the same effect, only I liked it, a lot. I forgot I was in my house.

When the song ended, (this is where things get fuzzy) she pulled me to the couch. At first, I tried to push myself off her, but she held me tight.

"I told you I had a birthday present for you, Tucker," she panted.

The next record plopped down onto the turntable. The urgent beat of Curtis Lee's "Angel Eyes" pounded in my head, and I dissolved. I was feverish, on fire, and I kissed her (I told you I had a fever). I couldn't stop moaning.

That's when I heard the front door open and Mom yell, "We're home." I rolled off the sofa and slid onto the floor, resisting the urge to crawl away on my hands and knees. I stood up just as Mom and Dad entered. June smiled and smoothed her skirt; cool as a cucumber. I was impressed. While they settled up (Dad said they came home early because Mom had a headache), I quietly snuck out to the back porch. June left, and Mom and Dad turned on the TV. And here I am.

Tucker closed the notebook, slid the pen into the spiral binding, and turned the portable radio off. He sat very still, but for how long he could not say.

"Did you have a nice birthday, Tucker?" Vienna asked, leaning her head out the window and startling her son.

He nodded. "Uh-huh. Yes, I did, Mom." Tucker paused. "Any cake left?" Then he stood up, walked in the house, and shut the door behind him.

Profile: Johnny Farina—Santo & Johnny
Interview: October 12, 1989

Note:

A mass weariness embraced the psyche of most Americans as the '50s decade wound down. War and politics took their toll. Sound familiar?

Yes, the times they were a changing.

The music scene was going through a similar evolution.

The decade began with artists such as Frankie Laine, Teresa Brewer, and the Andrew Sisters, but it gave way to Carl Perkins, Elvis Presley, and the Teenagers.

The instrumental group emerged as a spoke on the rolling wheel of Rock music. Duane Eddy, Link Wray, the Champs, and Johnny and the Hurricanes became a common staple in the diet of American music. Of the fifty number one songs in 1959, six of them were instrumentals, and the ninth ranked single of that year was "Sleep Walk" by Santo & Johnny.

How was "Sleep Walk" created and titled?

"We graduated to the point where we started to write music without realizing we were writing songs. One night, after a job, we started to play, and we came up with the idea for "Sleep Walk." The only thing I seem to remember was that my manager wanted to know what inspired me to play this melody. Was there a bright moon out or something? I said that we started to write it at night, and we couldn't sleep. He said, "I'll call it "Sleep Walk." It was his idea. His name was Ed Burton. He also managed Bobby Darin and Wayne Newton."

What lead to your initial success?
"Around 1958, I decided that it was time to bring demos around to the record labels. See, in those days,

either I was a dreamer, or I thought that it was easier to be a Rock star. I knew that there were a lot of places in New York where you could walk in. So for nine-dollars, we recorded three sides in a little studio in Brooklyn. I started to bring them around to record companies. It took about six months before anyone would even listen to the songs.

"A lot of people would say to leave it, and we'll get back to you, or they didn't want to hear instrumentals. There was one man who did want to hear it and who was a publisher. Ed Burton. I walked into his office one day, and he was having lunch. He said to put the demo on; he wanted to hear it.

"He liked it and brought it up to Canadian American. Then Alan Freed heard it, and he liked it, also. The side that they liked was "Sleep Walk." The B-side was "All Night Diner."

Did your success change you?

"As soon as we had our success, all my friends came out of the walls like cockroaches. Everybody wanted to be my friend. My sudden fame didn't change me at all. It changed the people around me. They couldn't handle my success.

"First, all the girls that I wanted to go out with, and refused me, now wanted to because I had a hit record. I'm the type of guy that if you can't like me the way I am, then don't like me for what I'm doing. I couldn't handle that too much.

"A lot of my so-called friends would say, 'Here comes the star.' They seemed to be intimidated when they saw me. I never came on to anybody trying to be a star. People become envious of your success and instead of being happy for you, they become jealous, and it's not the right thing to do.

"Of course, I made enough to buy a new Cadillac, cash. It felt great, but if I went to my Aunt's house, and she asked me to take out the trash, I had to do it. I never, ever thought of myself as anybody special. I was just Johnny-from-the-block, only the block couldn't handle it."

What are your thoughts on the responsibility of performers?

"I'm from the old school. I think as far as the industry today goes, you have to be an entertainer, a preacher, and a businessman. You have to be a preacher, because if you have any influence over teenagers, I'd be trying to help them.

"I came from Brooklyn, and a lot of my friends overdosed on drugs and died. I never got involved with that. You can get high off the music. Your audience is looking up to you when you perform for them. So, if you're smoking a joint while you're playing, then you're giving off the wrong signal to kids. They would say if he can do it, I'm going to do it. That's why it's so easy for a kid to pick up a weapon and blow some other kid away. It's seeing all of the violence on TV and film. They become desensitized to it."

Partial Discography
JOHNNY FARINA: SANTO & JOHNNY
  "Sleepwalk"
  "Caravan"
  "Summertime"
  "All Night Diner"

CHAPTER EIGHT

Down For the Count

November, 1960

1.

The first snowflakes had drifted down two hours earlier, around four o'clock, just before evening rush hour began. The freak storm had already accumulated four inches, and there was no sign of a let up. Traffic snaked slowly east and west, along Springfield Avenue, the major six-lane artery connecting Newark, Irvington, and Maplewood. Two blocks north, on Stuyvesant Avenue, Tucker had watched a tan Volkswagen skid on an icy patch and fishtail into a boarded up news stand. A tow truck's emergency lights painted the storefronts yellow.

The ferocity of a sudden wind gust whipped the bus stop sign violently side-to-side and hurled a wall of powdery snow crystals into Tucker's face. They stung his cheeks and made his eyes water. *I should have listened to Mom,* he thought.

"Don't forget your rubbers and gloves!" she had insisted.

"I don't need them," he had insisted back. He leaned back against the metal bus stop sign, hoping it would provide some protection against the bitter cold and blowing snow. His face and hands were chafed raw; the snow soaked through his sneakers, and his nose leaked.

He pulled his knit cap lower over his ears, wrapped the wool scarf tighter around his neck, and shoved his gloveless hands deeper into his coat pockets. His new gym bag, crusted with snow, sat at his feet; Irvington Police Athletic League lettered across its top.

"T-Tucker," Kerry chattered, emerging from behind a curtain of white powder. He was bundled in a hooded car coat and carried a gym bag similar to Tuckers. "Sorry I'm late."

"Jeez, man! Where have you been? You know the bus is going to be here any second. You could have missed it."

"Have you noticed the weather, Tuck? It's just a little slow going out there, you mope." He pulled a pack of Marlboros from his coat pocket, fished a cigarette out, and lit it up. "Calm down, already. Are you sure the fight is even on?" He blew out a stream of blue smoke.

"Yeah, I called Max before I left the house. He said it would take the Governor calling a State of Emergency before they would call it off."

"This is nuts, man."

The bus turned the corner and eased to a stop in front of them. The doors opened with a whoosh, and they climbed on. They each dropped change into top of the automatic coin collection box and then took seats in the rear of the bus. They were the only riders. The engine whined in protest as the bus pulled away from the curb.

"Man, it stinks in here," Tucker complained, opening his window an inch. The inside of the bus smelled like urine and stale cigarettes, and the bus's heater amplified it.

"Is your Dad coming tonight in this weather, Tuck?" Kerry asked, opening his coat.

"Yeah, he's going to meet us there. He had to stop at the TV repair shop after work to pick up some tubes for our television."

Kerry chuckled. "My father says that television is run by people who can do nothing else and watched by people who have nothing else to do."

"Is your father drinking again? Speaking of television, did you watch the news last night?"

"No."

"There's this dress shop in London where they are raising the girls' skirts four to six inches above the knee."

"That will never last, believe me."

They rode in silence, bumping along the snow-rutted street, through downtown Newark, past Sears and Roebuck, National Shirt Shop, and the Newark Star Ledger building. At 40th Street, the bus turned right and slowed to a stop in front of a dimly lit red brick building. A lighted sign above the doorway read Newark Police Athletic League.

Tucker and Kerry exited the bus, trudged their way up the brick steps and through the glass doors. Once inside, a uniformed guard pointed them to a stairwell that led to the locker room downstairs.

Maxwell "Max" Cohen, the former P.A.L. New Jersey State Heavyweight Champion, and current Irvington Police Detective, stood in front of Tucker's locker. At 6'5" and 235 pounds, he was an imposing and well-muscled man. Movie star handsome, Max had decided to retire from amateur boxing (and getting his brains rattled) and train the "up and comers" for the Irvington Police Athletic League team.

Eight weeks ago, just after Labor Day, a Mister Farmer Pitts contacted him and insisted that his son be trained in self-defense. When Max first met Tucker, it was evident that, although he still carried a few extra pounds, he had been on a physical exercise regimen. The boy had a determined eye; Max saw that right away and agreed to take him on as his student.

Tucker displayed a quick grasp of the "sweet science," and he trained tirelessly. Every day after school, he went to the gym and jumped rope, practiced his left jab until he thought his arm was going to fall off, hit the heavy bag, hit the speed bag, and then boxed two rounds with Max. Bob, weave, jab, uppercut, right cross, clinch. He developed fast hand and foot speed fighting against his heavyweight trainer. It was good. It felt good. He was ready.

"Hey, Max!" Tucker said, sitting down in front of his locker. He quickly undressed and got into his shorts and t-shirt.

"Ok, Tucker," said Max, wrapping his fighter's hands, "I heard that the kid you're fighting is good. But you're good, too. Do not forget to be patient. Watch for an opportunity to slip his jab, double up on your own jab, and right cross. Got it? Just like we trained." He wiped Vaseline on Tucker's eyebrows and cheeks, then slipped his head gear on.

"Yeah, Max. I'm good."

Tucker hurried into the gymnasium, ignoring the jeers of some hometown fans, and headed straight for the steps leading up to the boxing ring. He climbed through the ropes, sat on the stool in his corner and looked in the audience for his father. He was not there.

"Open wide," Kerry said, putting in Tucker's mouthpiece.

There was murmuring and commotion in the audience as the heavily favored opponent stepped into the ring. He was the same height as Tucker, only more muscled. When he got to his corner, he turned and spit at him.

"Oh, my God, Tucker. Do you know who that is?" Kerry shuddered.

"No."

"Look at his shoulders."

On the front of both shoulders of Tucker's opponent were tattoos of Shamrocks.

2.

Olympic Park overflowed with revelers, mostly from Newark, Irvington, and Maplewood. It was always that way on Labor Day, when the amusement park threw its annual "Goodbye to Summer Celebration." The event dated back to 1887, the year of the park's creation. It concluded with spectacular fireworks, which signaled the closing of the park until the following Memorial Day.

The sun was nearly down, but it was still warm; a sure sign of a lengthy Indian summer. Dark shadows from surrounding oak trees draped across the parking lot, and the circus animals' pasture. The amusement park was, otherwise, ablaze with lights from the Midway, and the thrill rides.

Nestled in a stand of maple trees was the Beer Garden and Picnic Grove. Dozens of green wooden picnic tables, littered with beer mugs and hot dog wrappers, were scattered throughout and filled to capacity with families. Music blared from a portable radio. Marv Johnson was singing, "(Baby) You got what it takes."

In a clearing, next to the picnic area stood the Bandstand. It was a huge pagoda, really, and the home of Capt. John Cardile's Brass Band. The fifteen musicians, clad in red, military-style uniforms, performed an excited arrangement of a John Phillip Sousa march. The summer was going out in style.

"We have to go home now," Farmer said to Tucker, Kerry, and Blanche, wiping beer foam from his lips with the back of his hand. "It's getting late, and Mom and I have to get ready to go see Don Cornell at the Colonial Room. And tomorrow is school."

"Can we stay for one more ride?" Tucker whined, sticking out his bottom lip.

"Please, Mr. Pitts," Kerry mimicked Tucker. "We want to watch the fireworks."

Blanche remained silent; instead staring at her father and batting her eyes.

"You can watch the fireworks from the roof of our house. But, if you hurry, and take Blanche with you, I'll let you go on one more ride."

"And watch her like a hawk!" Vienna added. "There are all kinds of weirdoes' here."

The three hurried out of the Beer Garden to the concrete walk that edged the games of chance, wheels of fortune, and the startling shots from the miniature rifle range. It meandered through Kiddy Land, where the music from the famous 80-horse carousel joined with the screams of patrons being jostled in the bumper cars.

They stopped, briefly, to buy Italian Ices. Then they continued past the Ferris wheel, and the Fun House, to the most popular thrill ride in the park, "The Jet." The wooden roller coaster was rebuilt in 1951, after a hurricane destroyed the 1924 original, the "Whirl Wind." It was fast and compact. "For the small plot of land it occupies, it is the finest roller coaster ever built," raved John Allen, renowned roller coaster designer.

Tucker bought the tickets and met up with Kerry and Blanche at the entrance ramp. The walkway was just wide enough to fit three abreast, and they hurried toward the roller coaster cars. A small line, maybe 20 people, stretched out ahead of them but seemed to be moving steadily.

"Get outta my way, punk," the voice suddenly commanded from behind them.

Tucker, Kerry, and Blanche turned around at the same time.

Three toughs, dressed identically in black chinos and sleeveless tee shirts, moved quickly up the ramp toward them. The leader had greasy red hair and a galaxy of freckles on his face. But the most prominent characteristics were the green shamrocks tattooed on the front of his shoulders. The other two lugs sported crew cuts and snapped gum. They stood two paces behind their superior.

"Back of the line, buddy," Blanche yelled as the three hoods moved past her.

The leader stopped, turned around, and walked back to Blanche. Before anyone could react, he ripped the Italian Ice out of her hand and dumped it on her head. The chipped ice and blue syrup slid down her cheeks and plopped on to her new white blouse. The three thugs whooped it up.

The larger Kerry intercepted Tucker as he lunged at the redhead. "Stop, Tucker! He's not worth it. Blanche is crying for God's sake. Let's clean her up and get out of here."

"Yeah, and munch on this, you homo," Shamrock sneered, grabbing a handful of his crotch. "Your mother, and your sister, too."

3.

As Tucker would later admit, he was surprised how calm and unafraid he felt, especially since this fight was his first for the P.A.L. boxing team. For eight weeks, since his training first began, he wondered how he would feel, and what would he do when the bell rang for real. Now he knew. The fact was he could not wait to get in the middle of the ring.

He stared across the ring at Shamrock, whose headgear was not entirely covering his greasy red hair, or his freckled face. This kid was ugly. Tonight, he would do his best to make him uglier. Tucker bowed his head and said a silent prayer.

"Remember, Tuck. Be patient with this guy," Max said, rubbing his fighter's shoulders. "He's undefeated. Wait and watch for an opportunity. Keep your hands up in front of your face and snap your jab."

"Ok, Max."

The referee brought the two fighters into the middle of the ring for instructions. He informed them that they would box three,

three-minute rounds, a whistle would sound instead of a bell, and that the timekeeper would strike two boards together to signal ten seconds left in the round.

When there were no questions, he told them to touch gloves and go to their corner. Tucker stuck out his gloves, but Shamrock spit on them. Then just as the whistle blew, Tucker saw his father enter the ballroom.

Shamrock charged straight at Tucker and threw a wild right that, if it connected, would have decapitated him. Instead, Tucker ducked under it and deftly moved to his left.

"That's the way, Tuck," Farmer yelled from his seat in the second row.

"I'm gonna kill you," Shamrock slurred through his mouthpiece, and charged again. He flailed away, but Tucker bobbed and weaved, narrowly avoiding a rain of heavy blows.

Tucker held his hands high, circling to his right. He was vaguely aware of the crowd, but he shut out the distractions by focusing his eyes on Shamrock's chin.

"You little piece of sh—," Shamrock slurred, throwing a sloppy punch.

He had been waiting for Shamrock to strike first. When he had, Tucker slipped the punch to his right and then snapped his jab at Shamrock's face. He heard cartilage break. Before his opponent could recover, Tucker hit him three more times with quick lefts to the forehead and nose. Blood sprayed on to his gloves.

When Shamrock rocked back on his heels, Tucker hit him with a right cross, and then a left uppercut. Shamrock crashed to the canvas, holding his broken nose, and Tucker had his first win in less than a minute of round one.

Kerry and Max raced into the ring and embraced him. "You did it, Tucker. I knew you could do it," Kerry yelled, handing him a cup of ice chips to suck.

"Way to go Tucker, a KO in your first fight," Max grinned. "But didn't I tell you to be patient with this guy?"

"I was patient with him, Max." Tucker walked over to Shamrock, still on the canvas cradling his nose and dumped the cup of ice chips on face. He bent down to where he could look into Shamrock's eyes. "Munch on that."

Profile: Marv Johnson
Interview: October 11, 1989

How did you become involved with Berry Gordy and Motown?

"I met Berry Gordy while I was working in a retail store in Detroit. He, and his wife, came in looking for music. I was rehearsing a young girls' group. I was playing the piano for them and rehearsing a tune called "Come to Me," which turned out to be the first Motown cooperation recording on the Tamla label. He asked me to come to his apartment, which was located in the ghetto area where we all lived. His wife, Raynoma Lyles Gordy, was very inspirational to me, and all of us in the Motown stable. She played the piano and was very enthusiastic about the songs. Raynoma solidified the Motown idea. We had a very family-like little group. We heard songs, sang songs, ate hot dogs, drank strawberry pop, and had cookies in between. We were just a very close, little, enthusiastic, youthful group that was very cooperative with Berry at that time. This was the beginning of Motown. "

What was so unique about the Motown artists and the sound?

"Well, it was Rhythm and Blues modernized. The tambourine sound, with the heavy R&B beat, with the triplets and things. Aside from that, it's a prolific black-oriented organization. It was unique in that fact. In the early '50s and '60s, anything that a black man did that achieved any amount of national attention was, indeed, a phenomenon. Before that, it was like

MARV JOHNSON

Ray Charles, Jimmy Reed, and people like that. A lot of black people laughed at their music, especially the youngsters that grew up in the urban north."

What launched you to national celebrity?

"'Baby, You Got What it Takes.' That song did for me what "Lonely Tear Drops" did for Jackie Wilson and "Blueberry Hill" did for Fats Domino. That's *my* song. That was the one that was responsible for the notoriety that I still enjoy, as a matter of fact."

What were your tours like?

"I was just really beginning to break through with "You Got What it Takes." I was the pioneer, the first guy. You don't experience the luxury that the other guys do later on, like Michael Jackson. This was the time I was riding in the back of the Greyhound Bus, along with all of the blacks, as we went south to our engagements. I was still going to the back door to get my hamburgers. I am proud to say that I'm part of this pioneer effort, but it was a very different experience than it is now. No one could come in and demand to have champagne put in their room. When we checked into a hotel, it wasn't *really* a hotel. It was Miss-so-and-so's house who had some rooms for the night. Even the bus driver, who happened to be white, he'd go downtown, eat, and sleep better than we did. These are not facts based on any bitterness; these are just truths."

What do you want your fans to know about you?

"I want them to know that I was very much a part of the building of the Motown legacy. I want them to now that, and I want my grandchildren to know that. I want them also to know that because I was on United Artists, they are not as familiar with me as they would be had I enjoyed the publicity that was built by the early Motown artists. I was with United Artists but being produced by the Motown people, and Berry Gordy, and recording songs in the Hits field, the same as the other recording artists.

"But when they made a big picture of all the artists, I was not in it. When they held the 25th Anniversary of Motown, I was not invited. I feel it was very distasteful on the part of the administrators, and the persons who produced the show, to have a Motown reunion and not include me on the show.

"All I know is this. I can't see why Motown would not be aware of me as a person, who is alive, and very much a part of whatever success they are enjoying. I was not in the position to demand or to ask anybody to invite me. I don't feel it was necessary for me to ask when Pat Boone, and Adam Ant were on the show.

"'You Got What it Takes' was a very influential record as far as the Motown success story is concerned. Who can say? I'm like Marlon Brando when he said, 'We should not concentrate too much on who was the best, but who contributed, and who gave their heart and soul to the effort.'"

Partial Discography
MARV JOHNSON
    "You Got What it Takes"
    "Baby-O"
    "Once Upon A Time"

CHAPTER NINE

"Camping? Really? But what if I break a nail?"

February, 1961

1.

Farmer slammed the front door closed with his hip and stomped the residual snow off his galoshes. He hurried into the kitchen and dropped the heavy bags of groceries on top of the Formica counter, next to an opened quart bottle of Schaeffer Beer. One bag tore, splitting the red A&P down the middle. Soup cans spewed onto the counter, and the new linoleum floor.

"Hi honey. Thanks for going to the grocery store after work." Vienna stood next to the cylindrical Maytag, head slightly cocked to the left to avoid the cigarette smoke rising from the Camel lodged in the corner of her mouth. She wore her favorite flower-print housecoat and was hand-cranking undershirts through the wringer. On the stove, chicken sizzled in the cast iron frying pan; an occasional explosion of fat splattered the porcelain finish.

"I'm telling you, Vienna," Farmer grumbled, retrieving a soup can from beneath the kitchen table, "if prices keep going the way they are, it will be impossible to buy a week's groceries for twenty-dollars. And if cigarettes keep going up in price, I am going to quit. A quarter a pack is ridiculous."

"Thank goodness we won't live long enough to see the day when the government takes half our income in taxes." Vienna fished the last of the Farmer's underwear through the wringer.

"Where are the kids?" Farmer asked, hanging his wool coat in the hallway closet.

"Tucker is in his room on the phone with Kerry, and Blanche is in the living room, supposedly doing homework; but in all probability, she's watching television. Why?" The washing machine motor suddenly thumped and whirred; water pushed through the heavy, black rubber hose and flooded into the wash sink. Vienna dried her hands and sat down at the table.

"... and here's the 6:00 p.m. WINS weather alert for Thursday night—clear and very cold tonight with temperatures dropping into the low teens. Put on the long johns, booby, because the hawk is out tonight and tomorrow night ..."

"No kidding," Farmer grunted, putting away the last of the groceries.

"... Saturday temperatures will soar into the low twenties with a slight chance of sn ..."

He turned the radio station to WABC. A young singer, named Ray Peterson, was crooning about "the wonder of you."

"Why did you want to know where the kids are?" Vienna asked again, skimming the headlines of the Newark Evening News.

"Because I have something to talk to you about, and I don't want them to hear it now."

Vienna closed the newspaper and turned towards her husband. "It sounds serious, Farmer. What is it?"

"Well, you know the winter camping trip Tucker and I are going on this weekend? I was wondering how you and Blanche might feel about going with us?"

Vienna paused and stared at Farmer. She shook another cigarette from the pack, lit it, and blew out a stream of smoke. "You're kidding me, right?"

"No, Vienna, I'm serious. It will be fun with the entire family. We can go for a walk in the woods, fish in the lake, and cook our coffee on the wood-burning stove."

"In this freezing cold? Me? Traipsing around in the forest? Please. I play the piano for God's sake."

"Come on, Vi! Be a sport. We'll have fun. I promise. We have a whole cabin to ourselves."

She paused. "Camping? Really? But what if I break a nail? I just did them. Besides, Blanche has plans this weekend with her girlfriend, Lorraine."

"Get permission from her parents. We'll take her along." Farmer sat quiet.

"They will never go for it."

2.

The outside temperature was 16 degrees, under a canopy of stars and moonlight. The heater fan was set on High, but the inside of the Plymouth convertible was only slightly warmer. Through the years, the rear, zip-down, plastic window had yellowed and cracked, and a stretch of the seam had dry-rotted. As they sped north along State Road 586, icy air seeped in through the rent in the material.

"Farmer, we have to get a new car. This is ridiculous. I'm freezing my as ..."

"Mom! Not in front of Lorraine," Blanche scolded. "She goes to Catholic school."

"That's ok, Mrs. Pitts," Lorraine giggled. "You should hear what my father says when the Yankees lose."

Tucker sat silently, in the back seat, huddled beneath a blanket with Lorraine and Blanche. He wore his transistor radio earpiece and faced the window so his parents or sister could not see the tears welling in his eyes. They would not understand what was going on in his heart any more than he did.

There were some songs, some mysterious combination of notes, vocal harmonies, and lyrics, which produced a feeling that could only best be described as pure joy. At times, it overwhelmed him. Currently, he was trying hard not to sob listening to Billy Ward and the Dominos sing "Stardust."

He felt, more than heard, the words to songs. They vibrated deep inside him, and the performers—not all of them, but just about every vocal group, especially the Negro groups, awed him. They seemed respectful and reverent. Groups like the Flamingos and the Dubs made him weep shamelessly; he shied away from the public whenever those groups were on the radio.

They made him feel, he supposed, like being in church, listening to the powerful adult choir sing hymns in four-part harmony. The voices seemed to be singing just to him, confidential, like the church at twilight.

He liked Buddy Holly and the Crickets just fine, and the Everly Brothers, too. In fact, Blanche and he rehearsed the song, "Dream," with two-part harmony, and they performed it at all the family gatherings. It still didn't do it for him like the other vocal groups did.

Then there were the other times, when the songs deepened the emptiness. Lately, even at a crowded party, he felt like he was on the outside looking in. To make matters worse, he didn't have a girlfriend. He was fifteen, going on sixteen, and not a girl flirted with him. Not one girl had sent him a "Be My Valentine" card.

Didn't Aunt Louise just tell me last weekend at the family Sunday dinner that I looked like a movie star, Tucker recalled? Which movie star? Leo Gorcey?

He had shed a few more pounds, grew another two inches,

and was an undefeated PAL lightweight; but he could not connect with a girl. He didn't have pimples, either. Well, except for a couple between his eyebrows, but nothing like the craters on Kerry's face. So what then?

Maybe I am trying too hard, he thought. I definitely do not want a repeat of the Sandy Kubinek fiasco.

Farmer slowed the car and turned right off the state highway, and onto a two-lane blacktop that snaked alongside the north face the Ramapo Mountain Range; a ninety-minute drive northwest of New York City. The Plymouth's headlights swept the base of the mountains, lighting up an immense forest of barren, snow-covered oak trees. The gnarled limbs stretched in every direction, and when the wind blew, appeared to reach out and clutch at the air.

"How much f-further?" Vienna shivered. "I have to go to the bathroom. This place does have a bathroom, right?"

"Uh ... yeah," Farmer mumbled. "Sort of."

"What does that mean? 'Sort of'?"

Before Farmer could answer, Blanche and Lorraine let out a blood-curdling, nerve-shattering scream. "Monsters," they cried in unison, pointing out the window.

"For the love of God. What now?" Farmer complained under his breath.

"We saw things moving in between the trees, Mr. Pitts," Lorraine sniffed, twirling her hair and tugging at the plastic barrette that held it out of her face.

"It was nothing, Lorraine, just the wind. Now, unless anybody has any objection, I need to concentrate on driving this dark road. We will be at the cabin in a few minutes. So, please everybody just calm down." He glanced at Vienna.

"Having fun, yet?"

Ten minutes later, they turned off the highway onto a two-lane, deeply rutted, dirt road. It wound through a thick stand of trees and ended in front of the dimly lit front porch of a sizeable log cabin. A battered and faded metal sign, attached to the roof, announced "Camp Yaw Paw—Boy Scouts of America."

As Executive Director of the Eastern Boy Scout Headquarters in Newark, Farmer had to inspect all the camp facilities, annually, as part of his duty. He and Tucker liked winter camping, so it was a perfect way to do both.

"Ok, Farmer," Vienna danced. "I have to go. Light the lantern, bring the luggage to the porch, open the door, and do whatever it is that one does in this God-forsaken place, but show me where the bathroom is before I have an accident right here and now."

"Just take the flashlight, Vienna, and follow the path around to the back of the cabin, then head straight back toward the tree line, about thirty-yards, and you'll see it."

"See what?"

"The wood shack with the crescent moon carved on the front door. And here," he continued, reaching into a paper grocery bag, "take this along." Farmer grimaced, as if what he was about to do would ignite World War III, and then flipped a roll of toilet paper to her. "Don't waste any. That's all we have."

3.

The sun nosed its way over the crest of the mountain, edging out the night, and bathing the valley in the first soft light of morning. As the sun's rays inched across the land, the ground frost glistened, and the meadow sparkled like a diamond field. Somewhere close to the summit, and just beyond earshot, the enormous cat stretched, unsheathed her claws, and growled. She was hungry, and it was time to hunt.

4.

Blanche and Lorraine bounded down the wooden steps of the cabin, followed by Tucker, Vienna, and Farmer. The two ten-year old girls were linked together by a six-foot section of clothesline.

It was tied securely around their waist. Lorraine insisted on it as a condition of her going along on the hike into the woods. Tucker and Blanche had experience in wood lore with the Boy Scouts, and Brownies. She was new to the forest and was afraid of wild animals.

The winter sky was a pale blue and stretched forever. The air temperature, crisp and brittle, barely hovered above the double-digit mark, but it invigorated rather than slowed the group. Behind them, smoke drifted lazily upward from the field stone chimney in wispy tendrils, remnants from the early morning fire now dying in the hearth.

The five plodded west, through patches of ankle deep snow, sometimes stopping to throw snowballs. It was eerily quiet in the surrounding woods, save the occasional *CRRAAACK* of an ice-laden branch breaking off a tree.

Vienna and Farmer carried fishing poles, and each had a creel slung over their shoulders. A half-mile away, an enormous lake, thick with bass, lay cradled at the base of the largest mountain peak in the range. The plan was for the two of them to catch dinner, while the kids hiked the trail that stretched several hundred feet up the side of the mountain face.

Tucker and Farmer had walked it dozens of times and knew it would be safe, if the children hugged the wall. Besides, the height offered a spectacular view of the woods, lake, and valley below.

In minutes, the five reached the eastern shore. Farmer and Vienna dumped their gear and prepared to fish. Tucker, Blanche, and Lorraine sprinted to the path.

"Be careful, you three," Vienna cautioned and waved as they disappeared behind the trees.

"Not to worry, Vienna. The trail they're hiking just doubles back in a loop and leads back down the way they came from."

The two chopped holes in the ice and fished in silence, each caught up in the grandeur of the morning. The stillness of the frozen lake spread out before them. No words could enrich the stunning beauty. Time lost any meaning in this temporary world. Their reverie stretched on, enhanced by the numerous bass now stuffing their creels; but for how long, they would not recall.

Then the stillness shattered entirely, when the screams echoed off the mountainside.

When Farmer was sixteen, growing up in western Pennsylvania, he played wide receiver for the Ford City High School football team. He was lightning fast, earning him the nickname "rabbit." His acceleration off the line of scrimmage amazed everyone. His wife, Vienna, had only heard the stories, but now she witnessed it firsthand.

Before she could react to the shrieks, Farmer ran out from underneath his fishing hat, and was easily thirty-yards in front of her. His fishing pole lay where he dropped it. She would later admit that for an instant, the entire episode seemed like it was part of a Saturday morning cartoon, where a scared Sylvester the Cat runs right out of his skin. Vienna watched her husband disappear up the trail and around the tree line.

Farmer whizzed through trees, leaping over fallen logs in his path. Just ahead, over a slight rise, the frantic yelling had eased to an audible whimper. He skidded to a stop at the top of the incline, not comprehending the scene before him. His heart hammered in his chest, and he fought the urge to scream himself.

Twenty-feet in front of him, Tucker stood frozen still, in the middle of the path, facing the sloping mountainside. He clutched a thick branch in his right hand and was staring wide-eyed at something hidden in the trees. Behind him, skirted by thin saplings, the edge of the mountain path dropped precipitously seventy-feet into the frigid valley below.

The girls were nowhere in sight. Farmer was about to call out, when the big cat moved out of the shadows and crept stealthily toward his son. Its ears lay flat against the bony skull. It bared its teeth.

Suddenly, the girls groaned. At first, Farmer still couldn't locate them. Then he saw the rope looped around the base of a tree, both ends hanging over the edge of the dirt road.

The mountain lion crouched, readying to leap, when two fat snowballs rocketed past Farmer's head and exploded in rapid succession against the side of the cat's face.

"Get away from my kids!" Vienna screamed, spittle flying from her mouth.

The cat howled, more in surprise than pain, then bounded up the hill away from the hikers.

Tucker, Farmer, and Vienna reached the edge of the trail at the same time and peeked over. Blanche and Lorraine dangled from the rope, each holding to one another and sobbing.

"Hold tight, girls. We'll pull you right up." Vienna's voice was calm. In moments, they hauled the girls back on solid ground.

Blanche explained how the mountain lion had snuck up on them. Panicked, the girls backed away from the mountain lion and fell over the edge. The rope stopped their fall. "Lorraine saved our lives."

Farmer and Vienna knelt in the snow and prayed. "Oh, no!" Vienna groaned, rising to leave.

"What?" Farmer asked, startled. His head whipped side-to-side. "Is the cat back?"

"No, much worse," she sighed. "I broke a nail."

Profile: RAY PETERSON
Interview: September 6, 1989

You contracted polio at age 14. How did that affect your schooling and influence your singing career?

"As I went on in school, with my time out for hospitals and such ... I ended up graduating a year later, because I was not able to make up all of the credits that I needed to get back with my classmates.

"I never thought much of entertainment. I never thought too much of singing before [the polio]. I thought it was for sissies, as I was very much involved in, and lettered in, sports. I did sing in the choir because I did enjoy singing. It was just one of the things I did. I never thought of it as entertaining.

"I had done non-profit type talent contests in San Antonio, done television in San Antonio and, years later, was chosen the Top Teen-Age Talent in a four-city area. I was asked by some talent people from California that heard me, that if I could get out there, they did a polio telethon every year with Bob Hope, and they would like to have me on the show.

"So I made my way out there when it was time to do the telethon. When I got there, I contacted these people, and they told me the telethon was cancelled, because the Salk vaccine came out.

"I lived in the back of my car, and people's homes, and started singing in contests in night clubs. I won just about every contest you could imagine in the L.A., Hollywood, and Beverly Hills area."

How did your recording career begin?

"My manager, Stan Schulman, took me to four different record labels and set up auditions for me. I sang live. I got four contract offers from four major companies. I liked His Master's Voice. RCA was always one of my favorite record companies, and I felt that they would do the job.

"My first record was "Fever," and that was in 1957. Several years later, Peggy Lee recorded it. Peggy called me on the phone, and didn't know what to do with the song. I said that I had Otis Blackwell's phone number, who also wrote "Don't Be Cruel," "Whole Lotta Shakin," and fifteen or sixteen major hits.

"I got Peggy in touch with him, and several months later, she called me up. I was in Las Vegas, and she was coming to Vegas at another hotel. She invited me over for her opening night and sent roses to my hotel. Three dozen red roses and three dozen yellow roses. She honored me by saying that my rendition of "Fever" got her excited about the song, and that she wrote some new lyrics, and it remade her career."

Do you get the chance to see any of your recording contemporaries from your "glory" days?

"I've seen what's happening out there. I don't see a lot of my friends really singing that great anymore. A lot of them are burned out, a lot of them are kind of used and abused, and a lot of them are dead.

"I was with Roy Orbison just before he died. We took pictures together; him, and my wife, and me up in Canada. He had become a born-again Christian the last few years of his life. He grew up the same way I did in a non-denominational church. He came from a long line of ministers in his family, eighteen straight

RAY PETERSON

ministers he told me. He was the black sheep of the family; but he did have a personal relationship with the Lord and felt that God had led him back to where he was, and that's why he had been starting to see the success.

"In fact, he said that he hardly ever got home; he was on the road most of the time. It was soon after that time that Roy got sick. It was his heart, and he looked tired but, my goodness, if I had to go out and travel all the time like he did, and he put so much into his shows, that he was really together. I believe, to a point, that he fulfilled part of his destiny."

How do you see your music contributing to our pop culture?

"My heart breaks for the world that can't feed itself and that can't educate itself. I hope to be able to help some way. I don't care if anyone remembers my name. I sure would like people to enjoy the music and for it to come back for years to come; to delight and have fun. I think that's what our music was about back then, and I think we're seeing a resurgence of that type music. It's not just the people from my age, but I think there are a lot of people that are thinking that way. In every area, there's good music—hard rock, country, R&B, and heavy metal. But some of it, you got to look a little harder for it.

"I am excited about this guy called Ray Peterson, and the people around him. I think the industry is going to be better off for having me back in the industry. If I have any success at all, watch for the steam and watch out for the exhaust."

Partial Discography
RAY PETERSON
    "Tell Laura I Love Her"
    "Corrine Corrina"
    "The Wonder of You"

CHAPTER TEN

The Butterfly Phenomenon

August, 1961

It had been two weeks since Tucker turned sixteen. At his birthday party, Uncle Frank asked him if he had felt any older; were there any differences between being fifteen and being sixteen. Inwardly, Tucker wanted to yell, "Heck, yeah, I feel different. Now that you bring it up, the air is sweet, colors are brighter, and my heart pounds wildly when I'm near a girl. *Capish?*" Instead, he just shook his head and said, "Nope."

Normally at family functions, Uncle Frank wore his teeth and his glass eye. It truly depended on what his wife, Grace, would do. If she wore her teeth, he would wear his. She had decided that Tucker's party was not worth the effort.

As it was, Aunt Grace eerily resembled Popeye's Olive Oil down to the hunched shoulders and bun; but it was hard to tell who Uncle Frank looked like, especially without teeth and an empty eye socket. Every time Uncle Frank and Aunt Grace smiled, Tucker thought his head would explode.

There were more changes than just this new urgency, he acknowledged. He was going into his junior year in high school, and that was huge. At last, he neared the top of the heap. Somehow, he had managed to bob and weave through two years of school relatively unscathed, and unnoticed, no matter how hard he tried to gain attention. Now he was an upper classman and, suddenly, the possibilities were endless. He admitted to Kerry that it felt as if "someone had thrown a switch, and all the lights came on at once."

Tucker could not wait for summer to end and for school to begin. He was excited about seeing Mrs. Cheval, the school librarian, and thanking her for recommending he read Ian Fleming's "James Bond" thrillers. The spy stories excited him more than his "Hardy Boys" collection and stoked an already dramatic imagination. He spent hours writing summaries of each book for her.

She had read some of his original work, and liked how he wrote; his "voice," she called it. "Don't be so flowery, and you'll do fine. Just keep reading and writing, especially in your journal." She also encouraged him to audition for the Senior Play. "You have a real gift for gab, Tucker Pitts."

Where before, he had just done enough schoolwork to get by, Tucker now had an appetite for learning.

The most bothersome and confusing was that he no longer felt a desire to stay at home every weekend. In fact, he looked for ways to avoid family functions. *What had happened*, he wondered? He used to look forward to Friday nights with Dad, watching the fights, rooting for one boxer or another. More than that, it was their special time together—"Pitts, Pepsi, and Pugilism." Nothing could be finer. Now, Sundays were for church and family. Weekends were for friends and girls, not necessarily in that order.

Are you lonesome tonight?
Do you miss me tonight?
Are you sorry we drifted apart?

The radio played softly behind him. Tucker sang along with Elvis, running the iron back and forth over his black trousers. Satisfied that they held razor-sharp creases, he slid into them, pulled the short-sleeved, Banlon shirt over his head, and tucked it into the waistband. He tugged on his socks, and then slipped on his Thom McCann, ten-dollars-a-pair, Italian shoes; first the left, and then the right—the left sock, left shoe, right sock, and right shoe. Sometimes, to break the routine, he would put the right sock on first.

Do your memories stray?
To a bright summer's day,
When I held you
and called you sweetheart?

He had never really been much of an Elvis fan, although he liked "Heartbreak Hotel," and especially his rougher "One Night." Yet he felt that "Are You Lonesome Tonight" was the most powerful heartache and best break up song he had ever heard. It made him want a girlfriend even more, just so that they could break up, and he could sing this song to her.

Tucker heard the phone in the kitchen ring, and then his mother's footsteps as she shuffled to the counter to answer it. He pulled the plug on the iron, and then quickly checked his hair and general appearance in the bathroom mirror. Not bad, he thought. His face seemed more chiseled than he recalled, and his high cheekbones were prominent. The knit shirt accented his chest and biceps. No sir, not bad at all.

Satisfied, he shut the light and leaped down the stairs two at a time, from his new, attic bedroom to the kitchen, one floor below.

"Tucker," Vienna shouted at the ceiling. "Phone call."

"I'm right here, Mom," Tucker snapped, entering the kitchen. "No need to yell. Who is it?"

Vienna covered the phone. "Someone named Nicky Boom Boom. Who is this person? What kind of name is Boom Boom?"

"It's Nicky Giambone, my friend from school. You *stunod*?"

"Hey, watch your mouth, Tucker," Farmer growled, raising the back of his hand. "You want a fresh one? Apologize to your mother, now!"

"I'm sorry, Mom," a sullen Tucker mumbled. "You're taking me to his house tonight remember? He plays the drums. Boom Boom is his nickname. Get it? Nick-name?"

Tucker chuckled at his own joke and took the phone. "Hello? Hey, Nick. Sure, man, I'll be there. Seven o'clock, right? It's six-thirty now, and we'll be leaving in a few. I'll see you soon."

Tucker hung up the phone and turned towards his parents. "Come on, let's go."

"Hey, not so fast," Farmer, said. "Tell me again who this boy is. Are they Italian?" Farmer pronounced it Eye-talian.

"I told you already. He's a kid at school that has a band. He heard me sing in choir, likes my voice, and wants me to come to their rehearsal because they are thinking about adding a singer to their act." Tucker droned on. "They live on Wagner Terrace, right on the Maplewood border. Good folk, just like you like them. So, I don't want to be late."

"Oh. Your mother and I are finishing our coffee and reading the paper. Go watch TV for five minutes."

Tucker muttered something under his breath and stormed out of the kitchen, slamming the hallway door behind him.

"You better change your attitude, boy, and watch how you talk to your mother, or you're not going anywhere tonight, much less driving the car!" Farmer hollered.

Tucker had been taking driving lessons from his father, and his Uncle John, who drove a 1956 Ford Victoria, three-speed on the column, since he got his Learner's Permit on his sixteenth birthday. His parents were allowing him to drive the entire family in the Plymouth tonight for the first time. They agreed to accompany him to his friend's house, then drive into Newark for an Italian Hot Dog from Jimmy Buff's, and return at nine p.m. sharp to pick him up.

"Good Lord, what's gotten into that kid lately?" Farmer said.

"He's just a little high strung, Farmer. I think all the talk on the news lately about atomic bombs, and that crazy Commie, Khrushchev, pounding on the table with his shoe and saying that he was going to bury us, and then Kennedy telling everyone that it would be 'prudent to build a bomb shelter,' has us all a little nuts. Don't you think?"

Farmer sighed. "I suppose, Vienna. Grab your bag and let's go."

* * *

Tucker eased the Plymouth to a stop in front of a two-story brick house, bordered by an impressive hedge wall. A 1959, silver Cadillac, with the biggest tailfins he had ever seen on a car, stretched out in the driveway. Parked in front of it was a black Lincoln Continental and, in front of that, a delivery truck. "Provenzano's Meats and Provisions" was scripted on the sides and rear panels.

The porch light blazed, and Tucker glimpsed passing shadows through the living room bay window. He thought he saw the curtains move and wondered if anyone was looking at them. The convertible top was down; his father sat next to him on the bench seat wearing his new snap-brim hat, and his mother and sister huddled in the rear, disheveled and complaining.

"You did a pretty good job driving, son," Farmer deadpanned. "The main thing to remember is that when you see a police officer standing on top of a platform, in the middle of a busy intersection, holding out his white-gloved hands and blowing his whistle at you, it doesn't mean turn left and continue on your merry way. That would mean STOP!"

"I've never been so embarrassed in my life, young man," Vienna sniveled. "To think that we were chased down by a county dump truck, its yellow lights flashing, the horn blaring, and hairy men screaming at us to stop and turn around, as if we were criminals.

I sincerely hope that none of my friends from Eastern Star were passing by and saw us."

Tucker sighed, opened the door, and got out of the car. Farmer slid behind the wheel, Vienna moved to the front, and Blanche lay across the back seat.

"I got it, Mom. I'll do better next time."

"We'll pick you up promptly at 9:00 p.m. Please be waiting outside." Farmer closed the door and drove away.

Tucker hurried up the brick steps and pushed the lighted doorbell. A moment later, the door opened, and a slight, attractive woman, barefoot, and in shorts, stood bathed in the soft wash of the foyer chandelier.

"You must be Tucker," the woman said. Her voice was low and thick; her tone was friendly. "I'm Mrs. Giambone, Nick's mother. Please come in."

"Nice to meet you, ma'am," Tucker answered, shaking her hand. Her palm was moist; her breath had a suggestion of nicotine and alcohol, but definitely not beer. From the basement, an explosion of drum rolls and crashing cymbals interrupted them.

"Everyone is downstairs. Come on, I'll show you where it is."

Tucker followed Mrs. Giambone down a hallway lined with family pictures and into the spacious kitchen. An opened bottle of anisette stood on the table, next to a pack of Pall Mall. Some of the liqueur had spilled into a puddle on top of the vinyl tablecloth. A cigarette burned in the ashtray.

She pushed open a door at the far end of the room, which led to the back stairwell that spiraled into the cellar.

At the bottom of the steps, another hallway opened to the left and expanded into a dimly lit, paneled recreation room. In the rear, two men sat at a plush leather-tufted bar that extended along the entire mirrored back wall. On a set of risers, off to Tucker's right, the band was setting up and testing their equipment. Nick spotted Tucker and walked over to him. His mother joined the men at the bar.

"Hey, man. Thanks for coming," Nick said, clamping a meaty hand on Tucker's shoulder. He wore a sleeveless t-shirt; his shoulder muscles rippled in waves, and thick, fleshy lips parted to reveal a set of uneven teeth bound with metal braces and rubber bands.

"Let me introduce you to the guys," he said, pointing out the members. "That's Doug Davola on Sax, Jimmy Massero on lead guitar, and Carlony Zambito on the Hammond B-3. My sister, Mary Elise, sings, too. Wait until you hear her do the Marvelettes' "Please Mr. Postman." She'll be here in a minute. Boys, this is Tucker, and this cat has a good voice. We're gonna have him sing one of our songs."

Tucker grunted, nodded at the musicians, and then he followed Nick to the bar.

"This is my father." He pointed to the man on the left stool, dressed in khaki work clothes. "Carlo" was embroidered in red, over his left pocket. "Dad, this is Tucker."

"What kind of name is Tucker? It ain't Italian, is it? I see you met Ida, here." He slapped his wife on her rear end. Carlo belched, flared his nostrils, and then stuck out his hand. "Pleased to meet you, kid."

Nick introduced Tucker to the band's personal manager, Joey Lemongello, a stocky, thick-necked man, who sported a pencil thin mustache and wore a gray sharkskin suit. "Nicky tells me you sing good. We'll see." He did not shake Tucker's hand.

A door opened behind the bar, spilling bright light into the room, and silhouetted a longhaired girl.

"Hey, Mary Elise, come here. I told you about this cat. I want you to meet him."

The slender girl came around the corner of the bar, backlit by the stage lights, and sauntered towards Tucker. Her hair tumbled in auburn waves over her shoulders, and the room smelled like Jean Naté.' The music quieted, and then stopped entirely by the time she reached Nick and Tucker.

"Hi, I'm Mary Elise," she said in a soft voice. "Nick has talked about you. I'm happy to meet you."

Tucker stared wide-eyed. "Really?" [*Is that all I could come up with? What a loser.*]

"Yes, really," she giggled. Her teeth sparkled; an Ipana smile.

As hard as he tried, Tucker could not move. He screamed, "Somebody open up a window. I just want to breathe." Yet, nobody heard him. Her impact was instant and the heat unmistakable.

So was the smoke.

Upstairs, while Tucker and Mary Elise sniffed around each other, Mrs. Giambone's cigarette had fallen out of the ashtray, and ignited the puddle of anisette. The kitchen tablecloth was on fire. The next day, the papers reported no significant damage.

Profile: Gladys Horton—The Marvelettes
Interview: August 31, 1990

You began your career in a girl-singing group at Inkster High School, near Detroit. How did it start?

"The name of our group was the Cassingettes. It was slang for can't-sing-yet. I made the name up because I felt like we hadn't had any voice training, and we were really starting off.

"We were doing songs by the Shirelles, the Chantels, and the Bobbettes; the girl groups that were already established in that era. But the song we did at the talent show was an original one written by Georgia Dobbins, the same one who wrote "Please Mr. Postman."

"Georgia was supposed to be the lead singer for "Please Mr. Postman." She went down with us when we auditioned. The only person who didn't go with us, who turned out to be with the group, was Wanda Young. She married Bobby Rodgers, one of the Miracles. The other girls were Katherine Anderson, Georgeanna Tillman, Juanita Cowart, and Georgia Dobbins.

"Georgia's mother was a single parent, and Georgia was the oldest of the children. She didn't know who would take care of her mother if we had to go on the road. Georgia Dobbins left the group before we became the Marvelettes."

Who named the group the Marvelettes?

"Now that I look back on it, Berry (Gordy) saw a great commercial value in the Marvelettes. They came

THE ORIGINAL MARVELETTES
(bottom Right) Lead Singer Gladys Horton
(Left) Wanda Young (Top) Katherine Anderson

to us and they told us that the Cassingettes was too hard to pronounce, and we went for it.

"People would ask us if he named us after Marvin Gaye. We asked Berry once why he picked the Marvelettes. He said, 'Because you girls are marvelous.' Yes, we were marvelous, although I don't have the money to show for it, but we were marvelous to him. Somebody would be marvelous to me, too, if they would come in here and put my book all over the world. That's what we did for Berry.

"We put "Please Mr. Postman," being a song about a postal carrier, who is a very universal thing, and letters which are a universal thing. The postal carrier you can find everywhere. Anybody could relate to a letter, even if they can't speak English. If you pass them a letter, they know exactly what that is. So, the record, and the symbol being universal, took his company and, suddenly, Motown was everywhere. Before that, it was known only in certain states."

It has been said that Motown started, as a "family," and that you were part of it.

I'll tell you what we were part of. To me, Berry didn't do this. Everybody had a part in it. Everybody wants to say, 'I did it all.' Like Smokey (Robinson) wants to say that he was the company, and he wasn't.

"It was like a divine force moving like magnets to try and establish something. Maybe something that never had been done to see how it would be. So, Berry was in there because he had the company. Then came the drawing of the people.

"The Supremes were down there. They were down there before anybody else, although they didn't get a hit record out. Mary Wells drew people, and when we came, we drew people. It was like everybody who came there became part of this magnetic force. When you become part of this magnetic force, you go out and draw.

"Martha (Reeves) came as a secretary. She came down there because she heard of Motown and wanted a job. She thought that maybe she could get some of her songs out. Then they heard her sing, and that's how it started for her.

"It seemed like everybody who walked through that door, it was like a divine force that was trying to start something."

Were the Marvelettes Motown's first girl group?

"The Supremes were the first girl group. They were down there before us. They recorded before us. They had a song out before us called Butter Pop.

"We had the first hit record of the girl groups."

How did Motown treat you?

"We were treated nice. Smokey and Berry were tight. There was this little 'in-crowd' that you knew about. Smokey and Berry were that in-crowd, and it included anyone else that they wanted to hang around.

"They didn't come to us and say, 'Hey, let's party.' They kind of kept it behind doors. I wasn't one of that crowd."

What was it like to work with Marvin Gaye, and the Supremes?

"Marvin was a kind of shy person. When you did a show with Marvin, you saw him on stage, you saw him coming into the theatre, after that he was in the dressing room with his wife, and you saw him backstage. When you saw him, he always had a smile. I don't think I ever saw Marvin Gaye angry. He always respected Anna, and she was on the road with him mostly everywhere he went.

"Diana Ross, as a teenager, and you know how teenagers are, well, there's something about being a teenager that welcomes controversy. It's like if someone says, 'I want to fight you,' you say, 'Who?' Diana was different because she had something to fight about.

"She had been down there first, recorded first, yet everybody came down and got a hit record out before her. She had to deal with a lot of frustration.

"Mary Wells came down and got a hit record out before her, and she was there before Mary. Then here come the Marvelettes, and the first thing we put out is a hit, and we couldn't even sing. We could harmonize, but in no way did we have as much practice, or were we as groomed for the stage.

"We were clean, but the Supremes knew how to put that makeup on. They were city girls, and we were from a village called Inkster. So, we were like little country girls. When they first saw us, we were looking up to them. We saw their pictures up, and they were a nice looking group. Everybody had their hair done, and they just looked Entertainment. They had their makeup on, and their fingernails were done, and their lipstick was just right. Basic city girls.

"Diana was the type of person, just like at school there's always a bully. There's always someone telling someone where to go. Diana was that type of person. She would start an argument with you anywhere, at the White House, if you were there. She didn't care, and she had one of those kind of voices that when she started arguing with you, purposely she wanted everyone to know there was an argument going on. So she would get loud."

What went bad between the Marvelettes and Smokey Robinson?

"I had no idea in those days that Smokey Robinson

had a grudge against the Marvelettes. They made Smokey admit that "Please Mr. Postman" was Berry Gordy's first number one hit. It's on one of those albums that everybody is on, and he's narrating. He would say that it was "Shop Around" that was Berry's first number one hit. The critics had a different way of rating things. I even thought that "Shop Around" was the first. There was no argument with me.

"Every time someone would ask Smokey about it, he would blow up. He's the reason we haven't been on any of those anniversary shows. He's telling Berry not to be bothered with the Marvelettes, that they're all crazy.

"He figures I had the handicapped child, so I wouldn't do anything. He wanted us out of the way so that people would never give us credit, and if anyone did give us credit, we wouldn't be around to hear about it.

"I would be somewhere with my child, and there would be so many phony groups going around that no one would know who the real Marvelettes were, or even care. That didn't work, and I guess that's what really made me come back."

How did "Please Mr. Postman," and fame, change you?
"I don't feel things sometimes like other people do. It didn't really change me. That only thing was that I felt good that I had done something everybody was recognizing. I didn't feel like I was rich, or that it was going to last as long as it did. I said well, that was one hit.

"We were getting more attention then, and I had this feeling that I didn't want it to end. I just had no idea where it was going to go from there. So I just really worked hard at trying to make the group the best with routines. We had to be ladies at all times.

"I was very cooperative with the company. Everybody would get on those tours, and they would behave themselves. There wasn't a lot of bickering and stuff. It was just a lot of fun. I had more money to do things with, more than the average teenager did. It wasn't a lot of money, but I could go shopping more. I think I felt very happy that I was doing something."

Partial Discography
GLADYS HORTON: THE MARVELETTES
- "Please Mr. Postman"
- "Too Many Fish in the Sea"
- "Beechwood 4-5789"
- "Forever"

CHAPTER ELEVEN

Mary Elise Giambone

January, 1962

1.

Tucker peeked through the TV room's Venetian blinds, not because he truly cared about what was going on outside, but to avoid further conversation with Carlo Giambone. After two months of insults ("If you're not Italian, you're crap."), Tucker had finally gotten the message and decided to ignore him.

Well, that had its limits, too, especially when Mr. Giambone bragged incessantly about Nicky's band, Cold Cuts, and never had a good thing to say about Tucker's vocal group. Last Tuesday night, after a tiring rehearsal, Mr. "G" told Tucker that he was lucky to have Cold Cuts as the back-up band for the concert. Tucker questioned Mr. Giambone about his "gray matter." That caused sporadic laughter from the other men assembled around the Rec Room bar.

There were always men at the Giambone's house; some Tucker

knew, but some were different every week. Carlo told him that they were "trainees in the meat-cutting business."

Ida Giambone was pleasant enough, particularly when she had a couple of glasses of red wine in her, which she usually did. She was attentive to Carlo, and always dressed to the nines when her husband's friends were at the house, often cooking pasta, sausage, and meatballs for the weekly gatherings. A fresh pot of coffee continually warmed on her stove.

She was the Italian June Cleaver; he was the Neanderthal Ward Cleaver—heavy eyelids, rounded and hairy shoulders, and a stomach that sagged over his belt.

Tucker secretly thought that behind the make-up, and the clothes, and the jewelry, she was a sad woman. Maybe it was because of the way the corners of her mouth turned down or maybe it was because the holidays were over. He certainly felt low when the tinsel was off, and the Christmas tree lay naked in the gutter, waiting for the trash truck.

One afternoon, when he came to their house, Mrs. Giambone answered the door with swollen lips, and a bruised eye. "I thlipped in the thower," was all she could say or would say, through a distended jaw.

It was only five o'clock but already dark outside. Lights blazed in neighboring duplexes; Christmas wreaths sagged on two front doors. The streetlamps had blinked on a half-hour earlier, lighting an empty road and the dirty remnants of an earlier snowfall.

Still, it was clear and dry and posed little threat to Saturday night traffic. The church recreation hall will be crowded, Tucker thought. There weren't any excuses for people not to come.

"Alright, where is Mary Elise? We gotta go, already." Carlo pulled the pocket watch from his vest and snapped open the gold cover. "It's almost five-thirty. Nicky's gotta set up at six."

Normally, Carlo resisted all efforts to leave home on Saturday nights, instead flopping in his recliner and howling at Ernie Kovacs on the television. However, Joey Lemongello had promised that to-

night was "the big score." He had record company people coming tonight to hear Cold Cuts. They were going to be stars and very rich.

Carlo walked to the foot of the winding staircase. "Get a move on, young lady! You think you can get down here before the Commies put someone else in orbit?"

"Very funny, Daddy. I'm ready," Mary Elise said from the top of the stairs.

Carlo turned to Ida, Tucker, and Nicky. "You three, let's go." They all moved into the foyer; their footsteps echoed on the marble floor.

Tucker turned in time to watch Mary Elise descend slowly. She wore a black skirt that fell to the top of her knees, and a red long-sleeved blouse. What captured his immediate attention were her fingers gliding smoothly down the banister. They were long and tapered; each nail impeccably sculpted and tinted red. She wore no jewelry.

"You look so cool, Tuck," Mary Elise said at the bottom of the stairs. "Is that what the rest of the group is wearing?" She walked over to him and gently stroked the bandage on his chin.

"Thank you, and yes it is." He wore black trousers and shoes, a white, short-sleeved shirt, and a thin black tie.

"What do you two know? You think that's cool?" Carlo interrupted. "Wait 'til you see the jackets Cold Cuts is wearing. They'll make you guys look like you don't even belong on the stage with them."

Tucker never heard the insult. His eyes wandered over Mary Elise, lingering on her brown, almond-shaped eyes, then they lowered to his high school ring hanging on a chain around her neck. When he stared at Mary Elise, there was nothing else, nobody else.

"You look great, too," Tucker blushed. "You're wearing the same clothes that you wore on our first date."

She grinned. "I'm ready. Let's go."

2.

It had been more than a month since Tucker auditioned with Nicky's band. After the fire trucks had pulled away from the house (it was more smoke than fire), and the neighbors returned to their homes, the audition continued and went much better than he had expected. He sang the lead part of the Five Satins' "In The Still of the Night," while Cold Cuts sang background harmony. When the song ended, Joey Lemongello stood and applauded.

Mary Elise stepped up on the riser, grabbed the microphone, and sang "Please Mr. Postman."

Tucker thought she was magnetic. While the band shut down their equipment after the rehearsal, he huddled with her, each complimenting the other on their respective performances.

"I don't sing regularly with the band," she said. "My parents won't allow it. They let me sing in the basement. That's good enough for me."

"I never did anything like this, either. The closest I came was the church and school choirs and harmonizing with some guys in the Boys Room. What an echo. But I like singing," Tucker admitted.

"Tucker, your parents are here," Mrs. Giambone called from the kitchen.

"Oh, jeez, is it nine o'clock already?" Tucker groaned. "Ok, I'll be right up."

"Call me," Mary Elise said. It was more of a command than a request. "What lunch period do you go to?"

"Uh ... lunch period?" Tucker was still stuck on "call me." "Oh ... um ... I go to first lunch."

"Me, too. I'll look for you."

Two weeks passed. Mary Elise never showed up in the lunchroom. Every day at 11:10 a.m., Tucker walked up and down every aisle and scrutinized every table, but she wasn't there.

He hadn't heard from Nicky since the audition. That didn't bother him, especially, because fronting for a band did not appeal to him. He had discovered that if the voices and harmonies were good enough, they became their own orchestra. Still, he didn't want to force himself on anyone, especially Mary Elise, so calling her was out.

Tucker sleepwalked through his classes, and his grades plummeted. Otherwise, he filled his time with Saturday afternoon football, writing in his journal, and reading as many books as he could. Whenever he could find some extra time, he would squeeze in some homework.

On Wednesday morning, the last day of October, Tucker hunched over a bologna sandwich in the cafeteria. The lunch table was empty. Everyone who usually ate with him was either an officer, or the support staff of the Debate Club, or the Honor Society. Clubs, and most student activities, except sports, bored him. He discovered that he didn't mind being alone. In fact, he preferred it sometimes.

He sat close to the cafeteria exit. The noise from the students passing behind him in the hallway reached a noisy crescendo. A torrent of voices and sounds rushed in—

> *... that test was easy ...*
> *You sniffing glue, man?*
> *Did you see those hickies on Darla's neck?*
> *... kick the living crud out of East Orange ...*
> *Hi Tucker ...*

He swiveled around on the bench. Mary Elise stood in front of him. She looked electric in a red blouse, and a black skirt. Her hair was teased-up the way he liked it, and his heartbeat thundered in his ears.

"May I sit down?" she asked.

"Uh ... of course, yeah," Tucker answered. He shoved the last bite of his sandwich in his mouth and cleaned the crumbs from the tabletop with his napkin. He did the same for the bench seat.

"Here. Fit here," he garbled. His mouth was crammed with bologna. Tucker swallowed hard and wiped catsup from his upper lip with the back of his hand.

"We only have a minute before the bell rings. I have a lot to say to you. Meet me after school in the bleachers." She squeezed his hand and smiled. Then she rose and disappeared into the throng of students hustling to class.

***

Tucker leaped from his chair when the 3:15 p.m. dismissal bell rang, sprinted down the hallway, dodging thick pods of students, and burst through the glass double-doors at the end of the hall. He skidded to a stop in front of his locker, threw his books on the top shelf, and snatched his varsity letter jacket from the hook. Reversing field, Tucker bulled his way back through the glass doors and jumped down the stairs, two at a time until he reached the ground floor, and slammed open the metal fire doors that emptied into the rear of the school, adjacent to the football field.

It was a chilly afternoon. The marching band, uniformed in blue and white, strutted in precise movements across the south end of the field, rehearsing for Saturday's game against Montclair. The sounds of trumpets and trombones, field drums and sousaphones resonated against the brick walls of the school building. The football team began calisthenics on the north end; two captains barked crisp orders and counted cadence.

Tucker spotted Mary Elise sitting alone midway up the bleachers. She huddled in her brown camel hair coat, with a kerchief wrapped around her puffy hair. He waved, hurried up the steps, and sat down next to her. They smiled, uneasy; each stared out at the field.

"So, what do you have to tell me, Mary Elise?" Tucker asked. He was surprised at the sudden and mild resentment in his tone.

"You have a right to be upset with me, Tucker." A gust of wind grabbed at her kerchief, nearly whisking it onto the field.

She clutched at it and continued. "Please let me explain without interrupting me, and maybe I can get through this."

Tucker stared straight ahead and nodded.

"When Nicky told me about you, I didn't pay much attention. As far as I was concerned, you were just another upper-class jerk who thinks they walk on water. Then I met you, and you caught me off guard." Mary Elise sighed and turned towards Tucker. "You are a nice person. Your smile is gentle, and your eyes ... well, they are so green and alive." She took a deep breath. "When you had to leave, I was sad, Tucker. Imagine, I just met you, and I already missed you. I couldn't wait to see you at lunch.

"There was a terrible problem, though. I have ... had ... a boyfriend. We were on the verge of breaking up anyway, but I needed to put an end to it, for the last time. It wasn't easy, but I did it. That's what took so much time. I like you, Tucker, and I hope that you will forgive me." Her eyes welled up.

Tucker, still silent, took out the linen handkerchief from his jacket pocket and blotted a tear that splashed on her cheek. After a moment, he stood and pulled her to her feet. He leaned in close, as if to whisper in her ear, but at the last Moment turned her face towards him and pecked her lightly on her lips. They tasted salty.

"I'll forgive you if I can walk you home," he said.

Mary Elise handed Tucker her books, grabbed his hand, and led him down the bleacher steps.

The weeks flew by, each day a giddy new experience for Tucker. By Thanksgiving, his grades had improved, he was nominated for Junior Class President, although he lost by three votes, and his parents bought him his high school ring as an early Christmas present.

Every afternoon, after school, Tucker spent an hour with Mary Elise, at her house, watching American Bandstand. The nights were filled, after homework was finished and checked, with lengthy phone calls.

He learned so much. Her favorite color was purple; she loved pretzels and detested girl's gym class. The Shirelles were her favorite group, although she preferred Puccini's "La Boheme" when she felt stressed. In the summer of 1958, for her twelfth birthday, her parents sent her to Sicily to visit with her cousins. When she came home Labor Day Weekend, and for reasons she refused to disclose, Mary Elise swore that she would "never, ever go back there."

A week before Christmas, Joey Lemongello asked Tucker to audition for a vocal group that was forming in Newark. They needed a lead singer as quickly as possible. Lemongello had arranged for Cold Cuts to perform for record company executives at a church dance in January, and he wanted to promote the vocal group, yet unnamed, as well. He was convinced that the rest of the group would like Tucker's voice, especially his falsetto, as much as he did.

They did. As an audition piece, the group members asked him to sing the lead part of the Student's "So Young," an important song in an A Capella repertoire.

Tucker surprised himself with his command of, and confidence in his voice, and the ease in which he performed in front of strangers. After one song, they asked Tucker to be their tenor and lead singer.

Since the group rehearsed at the apartment of group member Anthony Apece, located on the corner of Avon Avenue and 16th Street, they decided to call themselves The Boys of Avon Avenue.

On Friday afternoon, the day before the dance, Mary Elise and Tucker leaned against a wooden railing, attached to an opaque glass wall which ran the length of the hallway outside of her dentist's office. Dr. Antonio Scarpetta, DDS, was scripted in gold leaf across the front of the glass window.

Early for her 3:45 p.m. appointment, Tucker and Mary Elise giggled about the day's events and talked in hushed tones about the possibilities that tomorrow night's church dance presented. During a lull in the conversation, Tucker asked Mary Elise to be his steady girlfriend and wear his school ring on a chain around her neck. Excited, she bumped him hard with her hip and screamed, "Yes!"

Unfortunately, the next sound they heard was the wooden railing splintering and then giving way. The weight and force of the two teenagers propelled them through the glass wall and into the Waiting Room of the dentist's office. Long panels of milky, corrugated glass exploded everywhere. Horrified patients screamed and scattered to avoid serious injury. Tucker and Mary Elise curled into a fetal position on the floor.

In slow motion, Tucker lifted his head just in time to watch a thin wedge of glass tumble end over end and slice through the bottom of his chin. Suddenly, blood was everywhere.

The dentist ran into the Waiting Room and applied pressure, and ice, while his nurse called Tucker's mother. Two hours, and seven stitches later, Tucker walked out of the Emergency Room. A thick bandage stretched across his chin.

Miraculously, the flying glass had cut nobody *else*.

3.

The church's recreation room was crammed with more than three hundred screaming teenagers, a couple-dozen parents, and a representative from Checkerboard Records. Carlo and Joey stood in the front row whistling and applauding. The crowd, restless after dancing to records for the past hour, was eager to hear the live band. They chanted "Cold Cuts, Cold Cuts, Cold Cuts!"

When Nicky's band finally walked onto the stage wearing orange and black plaid jackets, the young girls shrieked. The musicians acknowledged the crowd, then erupted into a blistering version of Joey Dee & the Starliter's, "Peppermint Twist."

> *We got a new dance,*
> *and it goes like this,*
> *and the name of the dance*
> *is the Peppermint Twist ...*

The crowd twisted, gyrated, and sang along. In the shadows of the back walls some of the chaperones shook their heads and sighed. When Cold Cuts finished the song, the applause was wild and unending. The band then broke into a raucous version of "Tequila," and finished their set with Del Shannon's "Runaway." The applause was thunderous.

Tucker took a deep breath when the emcee called The Boys of Avon Avenue on stage. This was their first public performance in front of an audience larger than seven people. His head and chin throbbed, dried blood staining the bandage. The crowd was still boisterous when he nodded to the group, and the harmonies began. Then Tucker sang "In the Still of the Night." The audience quieted.

When they finished, The Boys of Avon Avenue walked off to a stunned hush. After a moment, from the rear of the room, a lone voice yelled, "Encore." Then another voice, and another, and yet another plea echoed until the entire dance floor shook with the frantic teens yelling for more.

Stunned, The Boys of Avon Avenue walked back on the stage. The hollering intensified. Without hesitation, Tucker turned to the other members of the group and whispered the title of their encore song. Then he sang his favorite song; an A Cappella arrangement of the Dubs hit record, "Could This Be Magic?" When it ended, he was dumbstruck to see girls with tears streaming down their faces.

After the dance, Tucker watched Joey Lemongello, and Carlo speak to a bald man wearing a gray suit. Good for Nicky, he thought; Cold Cuts was going to get their record contract after all.

Moments later, as The Boys of Avon Avenue prepared to leave their dressing room, Joey walked through the door with a serious look etched across his face. "Ok, listen up," he commanded.

The group gathered around him in the center of the room.

"I don't know what I expected when I asked you boys to sing

at the dance. Fill some time, maybe, and give you experience performing in front of a live audience, not much else. Simple to understand, right? Cold Cuts is my major league team, and you boys are in the minors, waiting to come up to the big leagues. Hey, but sometimes, things don't work out like you thought they would."

"We did our best, Mister Lemongello," Tucker sighed. "We're sorry we disappointed you."

"Disappoint me? What are you talking about?"

"You just said it didn't work out like you thought," Tucker answered, thoroughly confused.

"That's right. It didn't. I thought that Cold Cuts was a lock to get a record deal. But what do I know?" A smile widened on Lemongello's round face, and he withdrew a folded sheet of paper from his inside jacket pocket. "I had it backwards. This is a recording contract. The Boys of Avon Avenue are the newest addition to Checkerboard Records."

PROFILE: Joey Dee—the Starliters
Interview: November 7, 1989

Note:

On a clear, crisp, Florida night, at Joey's house, four men reunited after a 24-year separation. They were Joey, Larry Vernieri-tenor, Dave Brigati-tenor, and Carlton Latimor-organ, all original members of Joey Dee & the Starliters.

They adjourned to Joey's music room, where Eddie Brigati, Dave's brother and lead singer of the Rascals, presented a new keyboard to Carlton Latimore. Then they jammed. Joey, wife Lois Lee, and the original Starliters, rocked with the The Peppermint Twist. The evening ended when we all joined Eddie singing the Rascals, Groovin.

It was music history, up close and personal, and I was there.

Yours is quite a story. How did it start?

"We were working as a house band at the Peppermint Lounge in New York. We were booked there, originally, for three days. That was in September of 1960. The owners liked us and extended our appearance. We left the Peppermint Lounge twice during that time. Once, to go to a place in Somers Point, New Jersey, and we went to Montreal, Canada. We were a little ahead of our time as far as the Canadian public was concerned because we died a horrible death up there. Because of that, we went back to the Peppermint Lounge. We were working there in October, 1961, when we had some society people come in.

"The Peppermint Lounge was located on West 45th Street, between 6th and 7th Avenue, right in the middle of the theatre district. People had to go right past the lounge to get to their cars.

"As I recall, it was a rainy night, and several of them stopped in to get out of the rain. They heard us doing the Hank Ballard version of "The Twist," as a part of our show. We were a Top-40 band, at the time. Some of these people got up and tried to do "The Twist."

"Our normal clientele was normally comprised of sailors, hookers, and tough guys. Well, a newspaper reporter by the name of Charlie Knickerbocker was with them that night. He wrote about it the next day in his newspaper, and, as a result of it, more celebrities began coming into the club, and it snowballed into a phenomenon."

How did "The Peppermint Twist" go from a nightclub phenomenon to a hit record?

"We were working there when all these celebrities were coming in. It was so crowded, and there would be lines outside for blocks with people waiting to get in. We had several record companies come in. I knew that speed was of the essence because everybody would soon jump on The Twist bandwagon. Morris Levy, owner of Roulette Records, said that he could have the song released in two weeks. We didn't even have a product at the time.

"We met on a Sunday afternoon; Henry Glover, who was a producer for Roulette Records, Dave Brigati, and myself. Henry played the piano, and we started writing words to The Peppermint Twist. Dave did the arrangement and the background vocals, and Henry and I did the lyrics. It took us about an hour and a half to write the entire piece.

"We went into the studio the next day, and, initially, I was the saxophonist, and the background singer. I had two great singers in the band, Dave Brigati, and Roger Freeman. Unfortunately, the song, as we were recording it, didn't get the desired sound that Henry was seeking. He asked me to try it, liked the sound of it, and went with that version of it."

How did Jimi Hendrix become involved with your band?

Dave Brigati: "We were seeking a guitar player. A friend of Joey's suggested a fellow that was staying at a certain hotel on the East side. I remember going to the hotel, with Joey, and walking into the lobby and meeting this fellow with large, pre-Afro hair.

"He stepped out of the phone booth, and we greeted him. He had a duffle bag in his hand, with pink hair curlers, two pair of socks, a spare pair of pants, a guitar with no case, no amp, and he was ready to leave with us on a two-week jaunt. That was his preparation."

"I was introduced to him as Jimi James, but his name changed every hundred miles. First, he was Jimi James, and then he was Maurice James. The Hendrix part came out, but never in the sense that it was his real surname."

Joey Dee: "He was with us about eleven months. He was working with the Isely Brothers, and Little Richard, and he tired of that situation. I had a drummer with me by the name of Jimmy Mayes who was from Chicago. We were looking for a guitarist, and he said, 'I know this dude who just got off the road.'

JOEY DEE

"At the time, I was living in Lodi, New Jersey, and I said to have him come over, and I'll audition him. He came over to my house, with his stuff in my garage, and he played for about five minutes. I gave him the job. He was excellent. He knew every lick, and he played ala Curtis Mayfield. No distortion, very melodic, and pretty."

Dave Brigati: "I ran into him after he became the Jimi Hendrix. I sat across the table from him, at a place called Steve Paul's Scene, in New York. I was there for full ten-minutes, three-feet away, and he finally stared at me. He got tears in his eyes, and he said, 'Are you Dave Brigati?' I said, 'Yes.' I had a feeling that he took a deep breath and said, like, 'I'm home.' He was pretty well out of it, and that's all I'll say about being out late in a night club. He was a lovely person as far as I'm concerned."

You performed with the Beatles?
"We did an extensive European tour, in 1963, for almost the full year. The Beatles were our opening act when we were in Stockholm, Sweden. It was November, 1963, just two months prior to them coming to the states.

"We worked at this place called The Star Club, in Hamburg, Germany, where the Beatles achieved their first bit of success in Europe. They were unique; strange in a way that we had the suits and ties, and the high-water pants, and they had the long hair.

"They went on stage first, and the place was in a total uproar. Bedlam broke out, and they needed all kinds of security. There was some kind of magic there.

"Larry Vernieri was with us at the time and said that these guys were going to be big stars. I pooh-poohed it saying they weren't doing any original material. They were doing Fats Domino, Little Richard, and Chuck Berry. I said that they were a re-tread group. We got the original artists in the states, so how are they going to make it there?"

What effect did the Beatles, and other British groups, have on American Rock 'n Roll artists?

"It's not dissimilar to our dismantling the Third Avenue 'El' in New York City and selling the scrap iron to the Japanese and having them bomb us with it. We gave them all of this musical background, and they came back and wiped out just about every American artist with the exception of the Beach Boys, Frankie Valli, and the Motown sound."

Partial Discography
JOEY DEE: THE STARLITERS
"Peppermint Twist"
"Shout"

CHAPTER TWELVE

The Boys of Avon Avenue

April, 1962

Journal entry
Irvington, N.J.
Monday morning—1000
23 Apr 62

1.

Sun light should be flooding into my bedroom at this time of the morning. It's not. The window shades are all up (Mom's way of waking me), but it's as dark inside as it is outside. The ceiling light is of no use because the bulb blew last week, and Dad still hasn't changed it (I will if I must). The only light I have to write by, other than the occasional flash from a lightning bolt, comes from the table lamp next to my bed, and that's not much light at all—even with the sun.

It's raining hard; too hard, it seems, for this time of year. There are sheets and waves of water attacking the house, like a violent, mid-July storm, not the gentle April shower it should be. Windy, too. Something is rattling. It could be my bedroom windows, or it could be the phlegm in my lungs. I think it's both. I hope I'm not coming down with pneumonia again.

I'm missing school today, and it's probably not a bad idea, especially since it was Mom's. I don't like to skip school—no kidding—because of final exams coming soon, but I feel weak and tired, like death warmed over. Besides, school's over in six weeks, and my grades are good. After the dizzying weekend I've just had, I feel it is more important to stay in bed and write about my experiences than listen to boring teachers teach boring subjects. Ok, so not all of my teachers are boring.

This school year has gone by at lightning speed. One second, it's the end of the summer of my 16th birthday, and I'm asked to audition to sing with Nicky's band; the next second, I've signed a recording and management agreement with a guy named Lemongello, and I am in a singing group about to make a record. A RECORD! Maybe it will be on the radio.

In between, Mary Elise is my steady girl friend, I made the Varsity baseball team as the starting second baseman, and I am surviving my junior year. Heck, I am more than just surviving. I did much better than I imagined I could. I have a B+ average for the year, Mrs. Cheval entered an essay that I wrote about Grandpa's funeral in a state high school literature competition, and it placed second.

Now, as far as Mary Elise goes, between rehearsals, homework, church stuff, and my Saturday morning exercise regimen preparing for Marine Corps Boot Camp, I haven't seen *a lot of her, and I haven't spoken to her on the phone much, either. She hasn't been real happy about that. She said that I was "getting her Italian up." What does that mean? B*tchy?*

Friday, after school, I saw her standing in front of her locker talking to her ex-boyfriend, Dewey "Fazooli" Ciasulli. They didn't see me. He had her backed against her locker and was gesturing wildly with his hands, but I couldn't hear what he was saying. Then he leaned in close to her ear and whispered something. She pushed past him, and he threw his head back and howled with laughter; his lips parted to reveal a row of crooked, dull, and yellowed teeth (keep puffing those coffin nails, Looie). What did she ever see in him? I didn't have time to ask her what that was all about because I had to get to baseball practice. But, I surely will. Then, I'll go ask him.

So, that is how the weekend began.

After dinner Friday night, a weird concoction of leftover pizza and Mom's fried chicken, Dad, and Blanche, left to go bowling in the newly formed Father/Daughter League.

May I digress and explain that Mom suggested to Dad that he join the league to help him take his mind off Billy Boy, who had recently taken up residence at Eddie's Egg and Poultry Farm ("We conduct a Fowl business"). That was at Mom's suggestion. Poor Billy Boy.

I wasn't at home, but the way I heard it was that it had happened after a brief power outage stopped the clocks for two hours while Mom napped. When she woke, she thought it was earlier in the afternoon than it really was and decided to take a bubble bath before Dad got home from work. She took off her clothes, wrapped a bath towel around her, and plugged the kitchen radio into the bathroom outlet. She didn't bother to close the bathroom door since Blanche and I had plans after school with friends, and Dad wouldn't be home from work for nearly two hours.

Patti Page sang "How Much is That Doggie in the Window" through the tinny speakers in the plastic Philco sitting on the toilet lid, at a volume just loud enough to drown out the metallic clicking sound of Dad's key engaging the lock, and opening the front door.

Billy Boy had come to think of the bathroom as its private nest and had taken complete possession of the bathtub. When Mom tried to shoo it out of the tub, it went after her towel, pecking and flapping until the towel loosened and fell to the floor.

I can't imagine how Mom felt when she saw Dad, and his boss, Mr. Krauss, who Dad unexpectedly brought home for supper, appear in the bathroom doorway. They all screamed at the same instant, and Mom slammed the door shut, only to open it a moment later and fling Billy Boy into the hallway. There is a dent in the wall where he crashed into it.

Anyway, Friday night's group rehearsal was the most important of our limited existence. We had to tighten up the two original songs for the demo session, and for the recording session in New York Sunday night (I'll get into that Momentarily), rehearse new material for some upcoming school dance performances, and have some fun vocalizing on the corner with other neighborhood singing groups. The rehearsal and street corner activities were usually over by 9:30 p.m., and I was usually home by my 10:00 p.m. curfew. Usually.

Since appointed group leader (by the other members), and the lead singer on most of the songs (by Joey), it is important for me to be prompt, which I always am, early, in fact, to our rehearsals. So, after I finished drying the supper dishes, I only had 10-minutes to change into the new group "costume"—the blue-on-blue, Hi-Roll collar shirt, and charcoal trousers that Joey bought for us. The Boys of Avon Avenue were going to debut their matching outfits tonight.

I changed my clothes, brushed my teeth, touched up my

hair, splashed on some Canoe, and headed toward the door with three-minutes to spare. Except that Mom took that exact Moment to talk to me about my future, although I'm not sure whether she was concerned about mine, or hers.

"You look so grown up," she said. Whenever she has starts a conversation with that phrase, a monologue follows about how fast time goes. This time was no different, except that she added, "You look tired and run down."

"Jeez, Mom, stop worrying, already. I'm going in the Marine Corps next year. I'm in good shape, and getting better every day." I struck a Charles Atlas pose, but she didn't crack a smile. What I didn't say was that I did feel a little off center.

She continued rambling, as if she hadn't heard a word I said. "How are you going to get along in boot camp without me? Aunt Gloria is a nervous wreck that Cousin Charley is going into the Marines in June. It's dangerous out there, Tucker. Are you listening to me? Last month, Khrushchev said they have a better rocket to deliver nuclear bombs than we do." Then she retrieved the morning paper from the kitchen table and read "the good news" how Secretary of Defense McNamara felt "very optimistic that we were effectively curbing Communist guerillas in South Viet Nam."

What is a guerilla, where is South Viet Nam, and what, exactly, does "effectively curbing" mean?

I told her she was right about time passing quickly, and that I had to leave for rehearsal, or I'd be late. As I closed the front door behind me, I heard her crying about the recent tragedy that befell the Great Wallendas in Detroit, and how if it could happen to them with all of their training, it could happen to me.

2.

It's only a 15-minute walk from my house to Anthony Apece's apartment in Newark, where we hold our rehearsals.

The route to Anthony's is nothing spectacular, just a collection of zigzag turns every two or three blocks. The creepy thing is seeing the neighborhoods change from two-story colonials, with shuttered windows, and manicured lawns, to rusty warehouses, broken windows, and grimy brownstones. Even the air smells different—curdled, rancid.

Anthony, and two older brothers, Carmine, and Albert, live in a two-bedroom, first floor corner apartment bracketed by Max's Tavern and the Avon Avenue Kosher Deli. It isn't much to look at—over-stuffed furniture decorated with crocheted doilies, peeling wallpaper. His apartment is really more like a phone booth with a toilet.

I don't know if Anthony has parents, because if he does, I've never seen them, he hasn't spoken about them, and I've never asked. I suppose if he wants me to know, he'll tell me. What I do know is that, he always looks like he needs a shave and he doesn't like to be called "Tony." What he does best is figuring out the vocal arrangements for us, although he also has a strong tenor voice, and sings lead on several of our songs.

I should take this time to tell a little more about the rest of the group, and I will, but the truth is that I don't know too much about the others. We are from different cities, and we don't spend time together other than at rehearsals, and the weekend dances. We are all sixteen and love to sing, but Joey threw us together. It's not like we all grew up together, or we all go to the same school and sing in the boy's room. Still, The Boys of Avon Avenue's voices, in five-part harmony, are music to the angels.

Roger Hahn, tall and razor-thin, with scruffy hair and chin whiskers, is our second tenor and the quietest of the group when not singing. He nods his head if he understands something, or shakes it if he doesn't. Otherwise, he smokes Marlboro after Marlboro, and keeps his cigarette pack rolled up in his tee shirt sleeve, over which he always wears a three-button, black suit vest. It looks cool. I think he's the only one of us that will wear it with the new clothes.

Our Baritone is Freddy Testa, although his real first name is Frederico. He's a dimpled, square-chinned, big cat who wears horn-rimmed glasses. The chicks dig him. Freddy loves baseball. When I got to rehearsal (Five-minutes late. Thanks a lot, Mom!), he was squawking about how Giants' slugger Orlando Cepeda was holding out for more money. "Forty-five thousand isn't enough. He wants $60,000."

"Mr. Bass Man," as we call Paul Hahn (Roger's twin brother), is a serious student of the great Bass singers in vocal groups, and it shows in his performance. He's a big guy, too, with a heart-shaped face, and his voice is deeper than anyone I've ever heard, including the Bass in the Coasters; and, he anchors the bottom of a song like it was the Queen Mary.

He's a little too mouthy at times, and more than once, he nearly got us into a brawl with other singing groups. He kind of starts stuff, and then he smiles and walks away while the rest of us deal with it. Like all of us, Paul has a natural ear for harmony and the ability to hear a song one time and know his part.

I present The Boys of Avon Avenue.

We rehearse every Wednesday and Friday night and on Saturday afternoons. Our rehearsals are as intense as any football or baseball practice I've ever been in. There is no time for "any *@&#% chit-chat," as Joey reminds us. For three hours, less one 15-minute break, we listen to records, learn, and sing. If we finish our work early, we rehearse choreography. We warm-up by harmonizing scales, and then we dive into the first song on our list, period—no more discussions about baseball, girls, or school. The list is broken into "New Material," and "Brush Up." We try to learn two new songs every week, and then we rehearse the songs we previously learned.

There was no New Material at Friday night's rehearsal,

so after vocalizing, we ran through "Rock 'n Roll Knights," an up tempo number with a Sinbad-the-sailor flavor that I sing the lead on, and "I Won't Forget My Love," a bluesy-ballad that Anthony sings lead—and on which I sing falsetto. They are two original songs that Joey brought to us which we were going to record Sunday night in New York City and release as our debut record.

Our repertoire has grown, so the Brush Up list for the night was lengthy. It included the Orioles' "It's Too Soon to Know" and "Crying in the Chapel," as well as Dion and The Belmonts' "That's My Desire," the Passions' (and the Cadillacs') version of "Gloria," the Del Vikings' "A Sunday Kind of Love," and the Videos' "Trickle Trickle."

We breezed through the songs, each one sounding better than the one before it. There were moments, as I sang, when I wondered why we even needed a back-up band for shows, and recording. Our voices were an orchestra. By the time rehearsal was officially over, I was drenched in sweat but ready for some fun on the corner.

The Avon Avenue section of Newark is mostly Italian, and many of the neighborhood teens sing in a cappella groups—and they can all sing. I don't know when it started, but one of those group's members lived in Anthony's building, and he thought it would be a cool idea for the group to rehearse outside, every Friday night, weather-permitting, on the apartment building stoop. He encouraged the neighbors to come out of their apartments and be their audience. They did, the idea worked, and they soon developed a crowd of Friday night fans.

Another neighborhood group, and then another, did the same thing, setting up on their separate stoops across the street, with their friends and neighbors contributing food, soda, and encouragement. It turned into a weekly block party, which sometimes attracted a couple hundred kids, and, depending if the moon was full, or the Pepsi was diluted with too much Seagram's 7, a dozen squad cars.

When we filed out of Anthony's apartment building after rehearsal, looking boss in our new outfits, heads swiveled in the small, but growing, crowd. It was a chilly night, and I regretted dismissing Mom's advice to take a jacket, but it was worth it. For a moment, everybody on the block stared at The Boys of Avon Avenue, some even whistled; and, I felt great, euphoric, as if nothing, or nobody, could ever top this moment. Then, and I don't know if it was because of the excitement or because it was cold out on the stoop, or because it was a sign of things to come, I began to shiver.

"Stop him, Carmine," a girl's disembodied voice pleaded from within a throng of older teens to my right. Illuminated by a solitary streetlamp, they huddled beneath the canopy of a budding oak tree, barely visible in the shadows. Scuffling, cursing, then another scream, more urgent than the last, shrill, scared, "Sal! NO! Don't!"

By now, everyone's attention switched to the disturbance developing underneath the tree. Suddenly, the outer ring of the kids jumped back, away from the voices; their arms rose as if trying to defend an assault. Carmine, Anthony's brother, slowly backed away, too, exposing two lone figures.

Sal Barrata, at least 18, and a vo-tech dropout, staggered toward the retreating teens, swinging his right arm back and forth and mumbling incoherently. He resembled Sal Mineo in black, hi-top sneakers, with a jet-black, greased-back, duck-tailed hairstyle, and draped in a full-length, black leather coat. It sounded like he was either saying, "Mice are nice," or "slice and dice," which would make the most sense since he held a pearl-handled, nine-inch stiletto switchblade in his right hand and flicked it open, and closed. In his left hand, he clutched a clear plastic sandwich bag.

Behind him, sagging against the tree, was Camille

Andrucci, a pouty, 16-year old, red-haired, cheerleader from West Side High School, and Sal's current girlfriend. She was wrapped in a (you guessed it) black, leather jacket and painted into a short, tight, black skirt, under which she wore black stockings, and black ballet slippers. She was sobbing, and her mascara dripped down the front of her face in streaks.

"You pr-romised me, Sal, you lying piece of garbage! Put that knife down and give me that baggie!"

Then she screamed, louder this time, loud enough to draw attention from the neighbors. Lights began to pop on inside the surrounding buildings.

"I'm calling the cops on all you punks," someone yelled from above me. Yet, the crowd remained frozen-in-place.

Sal turned, pocketed the knife and weaved his way back towards Camille. He stopped in front of her, silent, and pulled a tube of Testor's airplane glue from his jacket pocket and squeezed the remainder of the contents into the sandwich bag.

"You're a pig," Camille hissed.

He grinned, wobbled, and then held the plastic bag in front of her face, taunting her. When she lunged for it, he snapped it away, pulled the open baggie to his face and buried his nose in it. Then he inhaled deeply, then again, and once more for good measure. When he finally lowered the bag, the physical effects of the glue were striking. Covering his brooding, brown eyes were silver-dollar sized, blood red splotches, especially dazzling against the rest of his face, which had turned from gray to a dull yellow, similar in cast to Dewey "Fazooli" Ciasulli's nicotine-stained teeth.

I never saw anybody sniff glue. In fact, I didn't know much about drugs other than I heard that some of the Negro singers smoked "reefer," and the rumors of some kids downing "goof balls" in school. I have no idea what they are. Kerry told me that Gregory Langham, a gaunt, but very popular classmate (especially with the girls), with an ever-present smile, ate them "like candy." Now that I think of it, Gregory does have glassy-eyes, but he is always nice to me.

Anyhow, Camille started sobbing, and Sal told her to shut up. She told Sal to do things to himself that really is not possible, and then Sal balled up his fist and swung hard at her head. Just like that. Only at the last possible instant, Camille ducked the punch, and Sal's fist slammed violently into the tree trunk, exploding into shards of bone, and a spray of blood. The sight and sound of it made me want to vomit. There was no longer a hand at the end of his right wrist, just a shattered, mangled, clump of flesh, bone, and tendons. Sal stared at it, but uttered not a whimper. Nothing. He took out a white handkerchief from his back pocket, covered the stump, then staggered across 16th Street, past the stunned crowd, and disappeared into the night.

Sal, by the way, is one of the greatest lead singers, of any vocal group, I have ever heard on the planet. His group, aptly named The Fumes, has a major reputation, not only on Avon Avenue, but also throughout Newark. His tenor, vibrato, and falsetto are unequaled. His voice is intimidating, and I could never understand why he hadn't gotten a recording contract. Now I know, and I am positive that he will be dead, or in prison, before too long. Sad.

Police sirens wailed in the distance (The old man did call the cops on us. Does that mean I'm a punk?), and I split. When I got home, and I ran home in record time, a blur, in fact, Mom and Dad were in their bathrobes, sitting on the sofa, watching TV. It was only nine o'clock.

"How was rehearsal, Tuck?" Dad asked, puffing on his pipe. It was cherry tobacco. "You're home early."

"It was harmonious, Dad, and I'm home early because we finished early." I hoped that explanation would suffice. It did.

"Did you have a good time with the other boys?" Mom followed.

"Yeah, Mom, it was a real bonding experience."

Dad chuckled. "Vienna, music is the glue that holds these kids together. Right, Tucker?"

"Good night, Mom and Dad."

"Good night, son," they replied.

3.

I woke up Saturday morning with a sore throat, and a bad attitude. At breakfast, Mom kept asking if there was anything else wrong with me, besides my throat. I kept telling her that I was just fine and to stop smothering me, especially the part about whether I could make it through Boot Camp without her. I reminded her that I was nearly a man and not her little boy any more.

That silenced her, and after serving hot oatmeal to me, and lemon wedges for my throat, she slinked out of the kitchen. I suppose I could have just told her I was nervous about the 11:00 o'clock demo session. I don't know why I didn't. The rest of the day pretty much went downhill from there.

The demo-recording studio was located on the third floor of a commercial building on Bloomfield Avenue, a bustling section in Orange, across the street from a gated cemetery, and next to a sprawling Safe Way Food Market. The bus let me off in front of the brick building, and I hustled up three floors to an outer hallway, where the group, and Joey, huddled against the wall, speaking in hushed tones. Directly across the hallway was a single, glass door. Across the top, painted in black letters, was "Diamante's Recording Studio."

I asked Anthony why we were hanging out in the hallway instead of going into the studio. He said we were waiting for the two cats that were producing the demo, and our debut record, to come out of the studio and bring us in. No sooner did he finish saying that when the door opened, and two men walked out.

The taller of the two was Bob Gaudio, and the other guy was Tommy Devito. Joey quickly explained (gushed is more like it) these two men were in a group called The Four Seasons, and their debut single "Sherry" was going to be released late in the summer, and that it was going to be a smash hit. Yeah, yeah.

They had us line up against the wall, shortest to tallest, then asked us to sing a verse of the "Glory of Love," a song we use in our live performances, so they could hear how our voices blended. They explained that today's demo session would help them tomorrow night, when "we construct the production for your hit record."

Satisfied, they brought us into the studio, careful not to trip over thick cables that snaked across the floor, and crammed us all into a postage stamp-sized vocal booth. We recorded the entire a cappella version of "Glory of Love" in one take, and despite my ever-increasing scratchy throat, it sounded first-rate. Then, just like that, it was a "wrap," and we were dismissed—all that edginess for three minutes of work. I didn't really care. My head was beginning to throb, and I just wanted to get home. As it turned out, that is where I stayed until it was time to leave for New York, the next night.

By 5:00 p.m., Sunday night, when I should have been bouncing off the ceiling with excitement, I was undeniably, irrefutably, and unquestionably ill. My head was swimming, and my palms, of all things, felt hot and wet. Given the importance of the upcoming event, I knelt down at my bedside and prayed that God would strengthen me, and protect my voice, at least until after the recording session. I also prayed for Him to send my Guardian Angel. It couldn't hurt.

I artfully avoided Mom and Dad, until it was time to leave for New York City, even convincing them that I had to stay in my room to warm-up before the recording. "Everything's A-OK!"

Mom usually had me vocalize with her; she played the piano, and I "do-re-mi'd" up and down the scales. This time, she didn't even offer. Dad brought a grilled cheese sandwich and a cup of Cream of Mushroom soup to my room.

I sat in the back seat of Joey's 1961 Lincoln Continental ("Six thousand dollars, and 5,000 pounds of luxury," he reminded us every ten-miles, or so.), scrunched between the Hahn twins. Anthony had the passenger side, up front, with Freddy in the middle. I love driving into Manhattan; cruising on the Jersey Turnpike, through the Lincoln Tunnel, and into the belly of the beast. It was different this time. I shut my eyes and slept until we arrived at the hotel.

I couldn't tell you the name of the hotel, or even what street it was on, even if Jack Webb interrogated me. It had the typical gray, stone, façade, glass revolving doors, and ornate lobby, trimmed in gold. And people. Lots of people. Someone yelled for us to "come this way," and I just followed the herd, into an even grander anteroom, outside a set of double-doors. Beyond, muted voices, and the erratic notes of tuning instruments, seeped under the doorway. My face was on fire.

When the doors finally opened, we entered the recording studio. It was definitely not Diamante's. Through the haze of my fever, the room, a rectangle half the size of our school's basketball court, reached out beyond the shadows. The overhead lights were off. A mini-lamp burned on the recording console, centered in the room. Three black girls were listening to the playback of a song they had just finished recording.

"Chains, my baby's got me locked up in chains..."

When it finished, they smiled and hugged. Their producer yelled, "That's a hit song, girls!" As they filed out of the studio, I smiled at one of them and asked her what the group's name was.

"The Cookies," she answered.

They are good, but I don't think their song is going to make it.

A four-piece band tuned up well behind the vocal microphone. Tommy DeVito sat behind a production console in a glass-walled soundproof booth, fiddling with knobs. Bob Gaudio showed us a wooden block, maybe 18" square (looked like the Parquet in our house) on the floor, over which a microphone squatted. He stepped on it, and began walking in place, stomping on it. He told us the sound from the wooden block, the same effect, was what The Four Seasons had used on their songs. We were going to use it on our record.

Tommy had us circle the vocal microphone. At his command, Paul's rich bass voice began singing, "Rama lama loop, de loop, de loop, bome, bome, bome. Rama Lama Loop, de doop, de doop, bome, bome, bome."

He was followed by the rest of the group, singing in five-part, tight a cappella harmony. The band began playing the music for "Rock 'n Roll Knights and Joey began stomping on the wooden block. This was it. We were recording our debut single, and I was singing the lead. Sadly, I don't recall much of it. My entire body was shaking, and the room was swimming. Amazingly, we recorded both sides in four takes. The playback was encouraging.

Again, I passed out, dead asleep on the ride home. Joey woke me when he parked, or docked the boat-like car in front of my house. I climbed out, mumbled good night to all, and staggered up the front steps. It was close to 11:00 p.m., and the house was dark.

I closed the front door behind me and tiptoed into the kitchen, guided by the night light that glowed next to the toaster. Quietly, I dribbled water from the faucet onto a dishtowel until it was thoroughly wet, and then I buried my face in it. It temporarily cooled me, and I draped the towel across the back of my neck.

When I opened the refrigerator door to get a bottle of orange juice, the refrigerator light spilled across the entire kitchen, lighting up the previously darkened side of the kitchen table. In the padded chair, nearly hidden by the opened refrigerator door, sat Mom.

"Sit down for a Moment, Tucker," she said. "Please." Her voice was gentle.

I poured some juice in a plastic cup and sat down. "It's not a beer glass, Mom." I don't know why I said that, but I don't know why I say a lot of things lately. Anyhow, it didn't matter. Mom smiled at my remark, and I felt the hardness leave my heart.

"We've been bumping heads, again, Tuck, and I don't like it. In fact, it hurts me badly, and I know it doesn't help you any, either. Dad keeps telling me it's a normal part of growing up, but I don't remember it this way with my parents and me.

"Shortly, much quicker than you or I realize, you are going to leave home for good. That's a paralyzing thought, if I let it take hold of me. I think that that is exactly what's happening to us. The problem is that Dad and I raised you to be independent, and now that you are close to being so, we, I, am having second thoughts. I'm terrified, but I'll do better, I promise. I'm proud of you, Tuck. But know this mister, despite your protests, I will always be your Mom, and you will always, somewhere in my heart, be my little boy. Give me a hug."

When I wrapped my arms around her, our cheeks touched. Mom recoiled as if she was jolted with electricity.

"My God, you're burning up, Tucker. Why didn't you say someth ... Oh, never mind. Quick, get upstairs and get undressed. I'm going to run a tepid bath for you. Stay in tub for at least 20-minutes, and call me when you're in bed."

"Yes, Momma."

The water was cool, but it felt good. I figured 20-minutes were up by the depth of the wrinkles in my prune fingers.

After I toweled off, I put on flannel PJs, and climbed under my quilt. "Mom, I'm in bed," I shouted.

Swiftly, efficiently, like a veteran doctor, Mom rubbed my chest with Vicks Vapo Rub, and then stuffed bath towels down my pajama top and around my neck. She tucked the quilt tight around my shoulders, bent down, kissed me on the forehead, and turned off the lamp next to my bed. "You are going to have to sweat the fever out, Tucker. I left a fresh, dry pair of pajamas for you to change into."

"Mom?"

"Yes?"

"It seems that I have been saying this a lot, lately, but I'm sorry. How AM I going to make it through boot camp without you?"

"You, my favorite son, are going to do just swell. Yes, you will. We are both going to do just fine. Goodnight." Then she closed my door, and the room went black.

PROFILE: Albert "Diz" Russell—the Orioles
Interview: August 12, 1989

The Orioles are counted among the top R&B groups in music history. How did it begin?

"I joined Sonny Til and the Orioles, as a Baritone in 1954, but I am only a second generation 'bird.' The original group got together around 1948, and consisted of neighborhood guys from the Baltimore city streets. Sonny had just gotten out of the service, and Amateur Shows were run in several of the clubs around Baltimore.

"Sonny won a couple, Alexander Sharp won a couple, George Nelson won a couple, and Johnny Reed won a couple. They won the contests individually. They said let's get together and form a vocal group like the Ink Spots, who were the inspiration for the Orioles. So, that's how the Orioles started."

How did the Orioles gain the national spotlight?

"One night, a young lady named Deborah Chessler heard the group and decided to take them on the Arthur Godfrey Show. They came in second to a guy named George Shearing. George won the Arthur Godfrey Talent Show, but there was such a furor across the country from the people who heard the show, and this was on radio that Arthur Godfrey decided to bring the Orioles back on his show for the second time. They hooked up with Jerry Blaine of Jubilee Records, which became the record company of the Orioles."

Who were the original Orioles?

"Tommy Gaither, guitar player. His relatives, and his daughter, still live in Baltimore. I run into them all the time. Johnny Reed was the Bass player. Alexander Sharp was the one who sang the high-floating tenor, Sonny Til, and George Nelson, who sang the second lead."

What was the first hit song for the Orioles?

"'It's Too Soon to Know.' Then they had a great deal of mediocre hits on the Black circuit.

"Many people don't realize it, but the Orioles were one of the first groups, as well as being one of the first R&B groups, to cross over into the White market with "Crying in the Chapel." I had the occasion to meet the gentleman who wrote it, and he was out of Oklahoma. The song was supposed to be a Country and Western song, with a foxtrot beat. Sonny slowed it down, and it became a hit."

To what do you attribute the Orioles popularity and success over 40-years?

"We have a market for what we do. Even with Sonny's death (Til died on December 9, 1981), the people wanted the Orioles to remain. When Sonny died, we were at the wake, and I looked out over all these people. I was the oldest, and I asked them what they wanted me to do. They said to keep on, don't destroy the legacy, and the legend. Keep singing.

"I decided that when Sonny died, and he did all the leads, that this was the end of the Orioles. But the people have encouraged us over the past nine years to continue."

THE LEGENDARY ORIOLES

RECORDINGS
CRYING IN THE CHAPEL
NEW YEAR'S EVE
TO SOON TO KNOW
TELL ME SO

Who are in this generation of Orioles?

"We have Reece Palmer, who grew up with Marvin Gaye. Reece was also in the Marquis and had the hit "Wyatt Earp." Chuck Battle is from North Carolina, and he's been working at this for about 25-30 years. Jerry Holman, and myself."

What are the Orioles greatest achievements?

"Two of them; when we were enshrined into the Smithsonian American History Museum, and when we were enshrined in the Billy Holiday Peale Museum in Baltimore.

"However, the absolute greatest was at Central State University, where they built a brand new museum, which is about a block long. We're on the video there six times a day. We were enshrined with Mahalia Jackson, Charlie Parker, and Duke Ellington. That honor brought tears to my eyes, because the curators said that this museum piece will be used forever.

"Who would have thought that when we began singing on the corners of Baltimore, that we would end up singing for Presidents and be enshrined in museums."

Partial Discography
DIZ RUSSELL: THE ORIOLES
    "Crying in the Chapel"
    "It's Too Soon To Know"
    "A Lonely Christmas"

CHAPTER THIRTEEN

"Thank you and good night."

October, 1962

October 22, 1962
Monday
5:00 a.m.

The alarm clock clicks ON as regularly scheduled, buzzing and whirring, shattering the stillness in the darkened bedroom. Trembling vigorously, the plastic clock shimmies to the edge of the nightstand. Just as it readies to topple, Farmer slams his hand down on top of it and squeezes the OFF button on the back.

He groans and lays flat on his back, motionless, while the fog of sleep drifts away. After a moment, he breaths deep—once, twice, three times in through the nose and out through the mouth. Then he blinks his eyes and wills himself to concentrate.

Vienna is still asleep, curled in a fetal position on her right side. Her breathing is slow and rhythmic. Good, he thinks. The alarm hasn't disturbed her. There is no need for her to be up this early. She will awake soon enough.

Farmer waits another three minutes to be certain then throws back the chenille spread, slowly swings his legs over the side of the bed, and stands up. Dressed only in a pair of white Fruit of the Loom briefs and tee shirt, he shivers and watches the breath explode from his mouth in cottony puffs; dimpled goose flesh crawls over his arms and legs.

He reaches for his bathrobe, which he always places on the top of the chest at the foot of the bed before retiring for the night. He sighs. It is gone. Dorsey must have pulled it off and used it for a bed. It would not be the first time.

Across from him, diffused light seeps in around the edges of the drawn, yellowed shade covering the room's only window. Farmer walks to it, pulls back the covering, and looks outside. A streetlamp blazes, lighting up the empty, rain-slicked street.

It is typical late October weather: plummeting temperatures and ugly skies. The leaves finished their annual color-change splendor weeks ago; most have now withered and curled into a brown, crunchy postscript. Outside, the wind whips and howls, sounding eerily like a child in unbearable pain.

Farmer tiptoes into the bathroom, washes up, applies Mum underarm deodorant (he detests having to dip his fingers into the white cream, and smear it in his armpit hair, but Old Spice Stick has too much alcohol and makes him itch), and shaves, careful not to nick himself. Today is not a good day to have his face covered with pieces of toilet tissue. Is there a good day for that? He slicks his hair back with a liberal amount of Vitalis and splashes on a handful of Old Spice after-shave.

Freshly laundered clothing hangs on a hook on the back of the bathroom door. After peeling apart the sleeves, Farmer slips into a heavily starched, white dress shirt. To complement it, he selects a silk, yolk-colored necktie, festooned with caricatures of children, and daisies, and deftly secures it with a perfectly tied Windsor knot. The black, pinstriped trousers hold a razor-sharp crease and break, precisely, two-inches above the cuff, over his highly glossed, black dress shoes. The matching suit jacket holds a lemon-colored silk hanky in the breast pocket.

After studying his image in the mirror one final time, he nods approval. He is ready.

Farmer closes the bedroom door behind him and eases down the hallway, past Blanche's bedroom, and into the kitchen. The room is awash in soft orange from the countertop nightlight. It is silent, except for the red second hand sweeping around the face of the wall clock.

Tick ... Tick ... Tick ... Tick ...

He finds the light switch behind the refrigerator and flips it up; the kitchen immediately brightens. After turning off the night light, Farmer digs around the cupboard, below the sink, and pulls out the blue metal coffee pot that he uses to make coffee on family camping trips. Five minutes later, it sits on top of the gas burner beginning to percolate. The aroma of freshly brewed coffee pervades the kitchen.

The tap-tap-tap on the back door is barely discernable, but for Farmer, who is a former Big Band singer and has excellent ears, that is hardly a problem ("I can hear a mosquito burp at 50-yards," he once told Tucker.) He glances at the clock—5:30 a.m. Right on time, he thinks, very admirable. Punctuality is the signature of kings. Isn't that what they say? He reaches the door in two strides and opens it wide.

Two men stand framed in the doorway, bathed in the solitary porch light. Both are massive in size. The one closest to Farmer wears a vintage 1940s police detective blue fedora hat, brim snapped down over his eyes, with a deep purple-black ribbon hatband, and matching blue trench coat. The other man wears a gray Bowler, the rim slightly upturned at the sides, with a small feather embedded in the hatband. He, too, wears a matching trench coat. Underneath the leather sweatband of each man's hat, written in gold, an inscription reads "Vigilance, Defense, Integrity."

Farmer steps aside and allows the men to enter.

"A great day, gentlemen," he says in a hushed, reverent tone.

"A great day," they reply in unison.

The first holds in his arms an unremarkable wooden crate, four-foot square, ten-inches wide, and secured at the corners with steel bolts and wing nuts. Although it must weigh several hundred pounds, the man handles it as if it were made of cardboard. Behind him, the second man carries in two green, metal suitcases the size of footlockers, ribbed in the center and secured with padlocks.

Silently, Farmer leads them to a doorway on the far side of the kitchen. It opens onto a stairwell that leads into his basement. Without discussion, the two men disappear down the stairs, careful not to bang their packages against the cinder block walls.

Farmer follows fifteen minutes later carrying a highly polished silver tray. It holds a pot of steaming fresh coffee, transferred from the campfire coffee pot to Vienna's finest silver coffee server, china cups and saucers, dessert plates, creamer, silver spoons, and linen napkins. In an ornately woven, wicker basket, lined with red satin, a dozen jelly donuts balance precariously, piled high on top of each other.

By the time Farmer gets into the basement, the two men have removed their trench coats and hung them on a clothes tree in the corner of the room. They are stylishly dressed in *identical natty blue double-breasted pinstripe suits with the same silk tie and wing tip shoes that Farmer wears. Both wear their hats.*

Two six-foot long tables, pushed together in the center of the basement, form the letter "L." A gold, linen tablecloth covers each of them. A bare light bulb hangs from the ceiling in the middle of the room and lights them up.

On the table in front of Farmer, sits a circular, monochrome monitor, three-feet in circumference, edged in a 24K gold band. It is obvious to Farmer that the round TV screen, as he thinks of it, is what came packed in the wooden crate.

Directly in front of the screen, perched on a cigar box covered with a gold cloth, is a red, plastic button the size of the collection plate at church. A platinum box encases it.

On the adjoining table to his right, a Sony reel-to-reel tape recorder revolves slowly. A console of switches and knobs, with blinking, tiny, green and red lights, butts up to it.

Freshly cut arrangements of daisies and sunflowers gather in cut glass vases at the ends of each of the tables. Connecting all of the pieces, a tangle of wires and patch cords droop over the sides of the tables and snakes along the floor to a wall socket nearby.

While Farmer pours the coffee, the two men slide into a secretary's chair in front of each table. The Gray Bowler puts on a set of bulky headphones under his hat and tunes the knobs, while Blue Fedora adjusts contrast and brightness on the round monitor before him. Abruptly, a picture materializes. It is the Mediterranean Sea, and only the three of them possess that knowledge.

"What is going on, Farmer?" Vienna thunders, suddenly appearing at the foot of the basement steps. Wrapped in her familiar terry cloth bathrobe, her face is puffy from interrupted sleep, and her hair spikes out at odd angles, but the scenario has gotten her complete attention.

"Good morning, Vienna." Farmer smiles, rolls another chair close to the monitor, and guides his wife to the chair by her elbow. "Have a seat, Sweetheart. I'll get you a cup of coffee and a donut."

"I asked you what is going on. Answer me! Who are they?" She nods towards the two strangers. The latter question resonates with fear, but she will not acknowledge that for a few more minutes.

The two huge men stare straight ahead, looking neither left nor right, instead focusing intently on their work before them. They have not uttered a syllable since their initial greeting at the back door.

Farmer, still grinning, slides his chair between Vienna and Blue Fedora. He sets a jelly donut on her lap and places her coffee on the table, away from the monitor. He glances at the screen and then turns to his wife.

"Well, you see Vienna, what you didn't know, and couldn't know, because of my Super Secret clearance, was that the Navy Department asked me," he quickly glances at the men, "us, the design team at Fillmore Metal Fabricators, to develop a small, light, and efficient thermonuclear warhead in the 1-megaton range that could be carried by submarine. We have responded, far surpassing our wildest imagination. This morning, we get to unveil our work."

"What in the good Lord's name are you TALKING ABOUT? YOU ARE A SALES MANAGER!" she shouts. The jelly donut rolls off her lap, leaving behind a trail of powdered sugar.

Farmer ignores her and continues. He is downright gleeful. "It is a rare honor, indeed, to head up such a life-enriching project. I present the Polaris program—sixteen compact missiles, placed vertically on a submarine and launched on demand without repositioning. The Polaris carries the first high-yield, low-weight nuclear warhead. Mark my words, Vienna, Polaris is a turning point in nuclear weapon design."

Vienna felt faint.

"As I speak, a submerged Polaris submarine is poised to launch a Polaris A-1 missile to explode a thousand miles away over the open ocean, out of the way of mankind. It carries a 1-megaton warhead. Not to worry, though, there is absolutely no harm to fish, fowl, or birdies." He chuckles. "You should be proud of us, Vienna. We're doing it for you, and the children, especially the children, so that their future is secure."

Farmer turns to his right, and without fanfare, pushes the giant red button. Unlike in the movies, no red lights flash, and no warning buzzers blare. Instead, all eyes freeze on the monitor's screen.

At first, in black and white, the picture shows the Mediterranean ocean, beneath a sun-drenched sky. It is calm with gentle swells, nothing unusual. Seagulls float in and out of the picture.

"Look!" Farmer squeals and bends in closer to the screen.

The sea roils, then a blunt nose cone breaks the surface; a sleek missile ascends from the submarine's womb into the sunny afternoon sky. As it rises, Vienna notices a picture painted on the side of the white rocket. Underneath the American Flag is a panorama of wide-eyed, chubby-cheeked children clutching daises in their tiny hands.

The Saturday afternoon air raid siren begins to wail outside; only it sounds more like a warning bell, like when the striped barriers drop at a railroad crossing.

Ding ... ding ... ding ... ding ... ding ...

"Oh. What's this?" Farmer's eyebrows knit tightly together. He studies the screen for another moment and then announces, "It appears that we have incoming. How did that happen? I don't know, but we will study this anomaly, and it will not happen again; I can assure you. This is not supposed to have *happened, incidentally. The computer model indicated as much, and let me tell you this, missy; there is nothing more dependable and reassuring than a computer modeling of the extremely complex phenomena involved in computer codes and nuclear explosions."*

... ding ... ding ... ding ... ding ... ding ...

Farmer places his hands on Vienna's shoulders and leans in close to her. "Rest easy, Vi. We use nothing but state-of-the-art computers, and for my money, the more powerful the better."

Vienna's head spins out of control and she gags.

"My concern is to understand the physics, Vienna. See these two contrails?" He points to two streaks slowly falling from the top of the monitor screen. "Those are probably Soviet retaliatory missiles that will reach us in a few minutes. In the 20-megaton range, I would speculate. Their trajectory, although somewhat elliptical, seems to indicate a slowing of the weapons, seemingly consistent with Breuhoffen's theory of minimal stress and drag. That drag coefficient, by the way, was my contribution to the project. We can only assume that they are about to discharge ..."

... ding ... ding ... ding ... ding

Vienna puts her hands over her ears and unleashes a piercing, primal scream, startling even the stoic bruisers at the tables. She recovers, jumps up, knocks over her chair, and flees up the stairs, taking them two at a time. "Tucker! Blanche! Wake up!" she screeches, then bursts through the front door and runs out into the middle of the street.

... ding ... ding ... ding ... ding ...

She looks upward; her head pans the horizon, searching frantically. At first, nothing, only the barren tree limbs whipping back and forth in the wind. Then she looks back to the left. Something freezes her stare, and she gasps. The earlier darkness has lightened a couples of degrees, just enough to make out the two bulky, misshapen forms that float down out of the purple, morning sky. They each hang suspended, swinging lazily back and forth, beneath a billowy parachute.

… ding … ding … ding … ding … ding

She estimates that the drifting silhouette, farthest away, is over Manhattan, which is only 17.8 miles from where she is standing. The other parachute, she notices remarkably without alarm, is currently settling directly over her at 2000.'

"Mommy!" Blanche screams.

Vienna turns to the voice. Tucker and Blanche, arms around one another, huddle on the front porch, their faces etched with confusion. Blanche's soft, pale blue eyes are red and watery. Tucker's mouth slacks open.

Then they are gone. Their memories vanish in the light. It is intense beyond humankind's ability to describe it. By God's grace, it registers in Vienna's brain for the briefest of moments. She never sees the mushroom shaped clouds ballooning up behind her.

… ding … di …

Within 1/1000th of a second, the fireballs form and envelop the cities. Temperatures rise to 20 million degrees Fahrenheit, instantly vaporizing every building, tree, car, bicycle, sneaker, dog, pony, and person. Anyone in underground bomb shelters is roasted alive as the bunkers are turned into ovens and suffocated as the fires consume all the oxygen.

… ng … ding … ding … ding … ding … ding

Vienna vaults out of bed, not yet realizing that she has awakened from a dream; her heart thunders deep within her in her chest. She whimpers and gasps. Beads of perspiration dot her forehead and drip in streams down her upper lip like spring dew. Then, as it always does, the nightmare begins to evaporate, taking with it every vestige of torment.

Well, maybe not always.

Sometimes, a nightmare is more than just terrifying. It is life altering, prescient, and resonates throughout the cosmos. It leaves behind an indelible mark, a horrific residue never to be erased, cleansed, or forgotten.

As her heart rate begins to back down, a memory resurfaces through the haze, confusion, and feeling of sick dread. At 7:00 p.m. tonight, the nightmare could be for real.

... *ding ... ding*

Vienna shudders and reaches for the annoying alarm clock, which is urgently trying to get her attention. Its 5:30 a.m., and, as it is every morning, Farmer's side of the bed is empty. His bedspread is turned down neatly, and the aroma of fresh coffee percolating on the stove drifts into the bedroom.

6:30 p.m.

Tucker hugged Mrs. Giambone tighter than usual, as if it were the last hug he would ever receive from her. They exchanged pecks on the cheek, and then he grabbed Mary Elise by the hand and led her down the brick steps of the front porch to his Dad's car, parked in front of her house.

At the curb, she lingered and looked back at her Mom. Then she stepped in and shut the door. As the brand new, 1962, midnight blue, Ford Falcon drove away, with the recently licensed Tucker Pitts behind the wheel and loud Rock 'n Roll music playing on the radio, Mary Elise waved 'bye from her window.

After a brief stop at the unusually empty Dairy Freeze for hot fudge sundaes to go, the two teens cruised up Clinton Avenue in the dark silence, each lost in thought. At Montgomery Avenue, they turned left and then made an immediate right into Tucker's driveway.

There wasn't enough time to get into the house before the president spoke, and they didn't want to miss a word, so they decided to listen to him on the car radio. Not enough time? The thought suddenly struck Tucker funny.

In seconds, the speech would begin, and the world would stop everything and pay attention. Tucker's unease was due more to his inability to control the situation than fear. Still, since there was nothing he could really do but listen, he was resigned and clear-headed.

Mary Elise was worried. She squeezed Tucker's hand hard, letting go only to shovel another spoonful of ice cream into her mouth.

When the radio announcer broke in, Cathy Jean and the Roommates just finished singing their chart-busting song, "Please Love Me Forever."

7:00 p.m.

Ladies and gentlemen, the President of the United States.

President Kennedy began.

> *Good evening, my fellow citizens. This government, as promised, has maintained the closest surveillance of the Soviet military buildup on the island of Cuba. Within the past week, unmistakable evidence has established the fact that a series of offensive missile sites is now in preparation on that imprisoned island. The purpose of these bases can be none other than to provide a nuclear strike capability against the Western hemisphere ...*

Inside the house, Farmer and Vienna sat in the living room, he on the over-stuffed chair with his feet stretched out on the matching hassock, and she in her normal position at the end of the sectional sofa, next to the pole lamp. They were drinking Maxwell House Instant Coffee ("good to the last drop") while watching and listening to the president speak on ABC-TV. He puffed on his pipe, and she opened the Bible.

Blanche sat cross-legged on the floor, feeding peanuts to Dorsey, who lay sprawled on his back next to her.

... include medium range, ballistic missiles, capable of carrying a nuclear warhead for a distance of more than 1000 nautical miles ...

"Can that reach us, Tucker?" asked Mary Elise.
"I don't know. Sssshhh," he answered.
Vienna turned to Farmer and asked, "Can they reach us?"
"They can't, but the Soviets can."

... striking Washington, D.C., the Panama Canal, Cape Canaveral, Mexico City, or any other city in the southeastern part of the United States ...

"That will definitely mess up Spring Training next season," Tucker deadpanned.
"You're already messed up." Mary Elise kissed him on the lips.

... jet bombers, capable of carrying nuclear weapons, are now being uncrated and assembled in Cuba, while the necessary air bases are being prepared...

"I told you this Khrushchev guy is a lunatic," Vienna offered between a sip of her coffee and a drag on a Camel.

... cannot be accepted by this country, if our courage and our commitments are ever to be trusted again by either friend or foe ...

Mary Elise tuned out the President and thought about her brother, Nicky. She wondered if he was doing any better. He had been depressed lately about his band's failure to get a record contract.

"I hope these Commies are paying attention," Farmer mutters.

... our unswerving objective, therefore, must be to prevent the use of these missiles against this or any other country and to secure their withdrawal or elimination from the Western Hemisphere ...

"Uh-oh, here we go." Tucker pulled Mary Elise close to him.

... we will not prematurely or unnecessarily risk the costs of worldwide nuclear war in which even the fruits of victory would be ashes in our mouth—but neither will we shrink from that risk at any time it must be faced ...

Vienna gasped. "Is he saying what I think I heard him say?"
"Yes," Farmer nodded. "It's put up or shut up time."

... I have directed that the following initial steps be taken immediately. A strict quarantine on all offensive military equipment ...

"Gloria is so scared, Farmer. She can't hardly eat or sleep since Donny and Charlie boarded those ships for God knows where. They could be floating out there in that blockade right now. In fact, I'm sure of it. Oh, Lord."

... should these offensive military preparations continue, thus increasing the threat to the hemisphere, further action will be justified. I have directed the Armed Forces to prepare for any eventualities ..."

Man, Donny and Charlie are probably out there right now. How cool. I can't wait to be a Marine. Tucker scooped up a large spoonful of ice cream and chocolate syrup and held it in front of Mary Elise. "Open wide."

... any nuclear missile launched from Cuba against any nation in the Western Hemisphere is an attack by the Soviet Union on the United States, requiring a full retaliatory response upon the Soviet Union ...

"Farmer, will you sit next to me," Vienna asked.

... no one can foresee precisely what course it will take or what costs or casualties will be incurred ...

"Are we really going to war, Daddy?" Blanche asked, rubbing Dorsey's tummy.

... the greatest danger of all would be to do nothing ...

"Come here and sit on the sofa with Mom and me," he answered.

... the cost of freedom is always high, but Americans have always paid it. And one path we shall never choose, and that is the path of surrender or submission ...

"You bet your sweet ass," Tucker pounded on the dashboard. Mary Elise flinched, splashing some errant chocolate sauce from the nearly empty sundae bowl onto her coat. "Oh, jeez, excuse my French, Mary Elise. I'm sorry."

... our goal is not the victory of might, but the vindication of right ...

In a quivering voice she asks, "Tucker, do you think nuclear annihilation hurts? I hate pain."

... God willing, that goal will be achieved. Thank you and goodnight.

PROFILE: Cathy Jean—the Roommates
Interview: July, 1989

You were "discovered" when you were 14-years old. How did that happen?

"I met a man at what they called a record hop through a friend in 1960, and my friend said to this man, 'My girlfriend can sing.' He says, 'So what.' As a matter of fact, he was managing a group called the Twilights, at the time, and he says, 'Ok. Get a demo on her.'

"After he heard that demo, he met with my parents and told them that he knew of two men that are looking for a voice 'just like your daughter's to make a record.'

"My parents contacted Jody and Jean, who later became my managers, and opened up Valmor Records. When they heard my voice, they said you're the one we're looking for."

They brought the song "Please Love Me Forever" to you?

"When I recorded "Please Love Me Forever," it had originally been slated to go on the flip-side of Tommy Edwards smash "It's All in the Game."

"I went into the studio and recorded it three times. They took the first take. It was released in October, 1961 on The Murray the K Show. They had a survey thing where the listeners would call in and vote on the record. "Please Love Me Forever" came in number two and from then on, it was a rocket sled ride to the top."

**CATHY JEAN
and
THE ROOMATES**
"Please Love Me Forever"

How did it feel to be so young and thrown into the national spotlight?

"To me, it wasn't really the spotlight because I had been entertaining, basically, all of my life. I was used to being up on the stage and singing. So, to have kids scream over me, I didn't find it to be impressive.

Having a charted record was new, of course, and I was thrilled to hear it on the radio."

How did you team up with the Roommates?
"I did not know the Roommates when I recorded "Please Love Me Forever." I knew there was going to be a vocal backup on my record, but I didn't know who. So when I went in to record, it was just the (studio) band and me.

"We became Cathy Jean and the Roommates, when I recorded "Please Love Me Forever." They went on to record "Glory of Love," and "Band of Gold."

Did you have to tour to support your record?
"Oh, we did that. We traveled throughout the Midwest. It was not very comfortable. There were all kind of one-nighters and then off to the next town.

"It was tiring. It was exciting when you were performing, but it was extremely tiring. I mean those buses were not equipped the way they are today. They are like floating hotels. In those days, 28-years ago, they were not like that at all."

What are you doing today? Plans for the future?
"We have been performing on and off. We're semi-retired. We've only done some big shows, like the Academy of Music, and the Westbury Music fair. That was a big thrill.

"We are going to perform full-time. The kids are all grown, and it's time for us to do our thing. I'm interested in performing and, yes, eventually recording."

Do you regret not having a more conventional childhood?

"Never. I could never be anything but Cathy Jean."

Partial Discography
CATHY JEAN: THE ROOMMATES
"Please Love Me Forever"

CHAPTER FOURTEEN

Tucker's Pitt Stop

June, 1963

As far as high school graduation parties went, given their significance in the life of the honoree, Tucker's was impressive; a Saturday-night blowout of historic and, some might contend, epic proportions. Not in the country club, faw, faw, faw world of crystal champagne flutes and caviar, and not that it didn't contain all the elements of successful parties past—music, food, guests, and ambience because those were there in abundance.

It had more to do this time with the celebration of *passage*. A place and time in one's life to stop, shake off the bad road, pray for direction, and gather up what one needs for the next move. A Pitt Stop, as Farmer referred to them, as did his father before him. This was Tucker's Pitt Stop.

The difference for Tucker was that this Pitt Stop represented the end of a life he had known for the past 17 years, and heralded the beginning of an entirely new journey, one without safety nets. He knew clearly this morning, sitting outside in the overhead sun with the other 643 graduates waiting to receive their high school diplomas, that he most likely would never see any of these people again. As each of the seniors paraded across the riser, Tucker realized that he really didn't even know most of them after four years together in the same school except to say "Hey, man," or "Great catch in the game," or "Watch where you're going, moron."

He had no particular feelings for any of them. That ambivalence, he supposed, stemmed from two things—his indisputable yearning to get on with the next adventure in his life, and from the dispiriting fact that some of his friends, especially Kerry, chose the local factories as their life's work.

Instead of a more exploratory pursuit, they opted for the daily afternoon Shuffleboard and "Bull and Beer" Dart League at Max's Tavern. Even today, while the thoroughly unknown Valedictorian droned on in an uninspiring speech, Tucker overheard Freddie Kincaid, Greaser Maximus, tell Joan Weatherby, Pastor's Daughter, that he'd like to teach her to "shuffleboard" with him. That realization sobered Tucker more than any lecture about the future ever could. He wished them well, but no thanks, not for Tucker Pitts.

Ralphie Amato, graduating solely by the mercy of the School Board (there is another Board in Ralphie's future, which will not be so merciful), said it best when he wrote in Tucker's yearbook—"Good luck and all that bullsh*t."

Tucker's teammates, his teachers, and the janitors were now a part of his past, not his future. They are then, and he is now. His eyes focused forward, not in the rear-view mirror. He knew there would be new friends, new experiences, and new mistakes.

As of noon today, he was officially a high school graduate, an alumnus; with that honor, and distinction, came the responsibility "to make something out of your life." The first test comes in two months; there will be a new residence—Marine Corps Recruit Training at Parris Island, South Carolina.

That isn't so bad, he thought. Tucker, in fact, was eager to leave his boyhood hometown, burning to see what waits on the outside of the little world he has lived in his entire life. It had been that way since the summer between 7th and 8th grades, when he saw an American Airlines 707 fly over him as he stood waist deep in the brackish waters of Cedar Lake, a tourist watering hole in the bucolic village of Beachwood.

As he squinted into the sun to get a better look at the gleaming, four-engine silver tube, his mind and heart flooded with questions and desires. Where has it come from? Where is it going? How does it stay in the air? What must it feel like to fly?

His Grandpa had the same wanderlust and regaled him with many bedtime stories of his travels, only he called it "itchy feet." It was dizzying. He didn't know how he would do it just yet, but he was determined to fly and to travel the world.

The answers, of course, were revealed to Tucker the next year when, awestruck, he watched Cousin Donny graduate from Marine Corps Boot Camp, and then last November when Uncle Joe invited him to accompany him on a drive to Camp LeJeune, the sprawling Marine Corps Base outside Jacksonville, North Carolina. Donny, and his brother, Charlie, were stationed there after the blockade against Cuba ended.

Tucker ate in the "chow hall" with his cousins and received a gift from their brother Marines: a Marine Corps sweatshirt that read "Once a Marine, Always a Marine," and a subscription to Leatherneck Magazine. There was no doubt about Tucker's future after that, except for the one Moment when Mary Elise asked him if he considered going to college instead.

The subject of continuing his formal education had never come up in any conversations with his parents about life after high school, but, because he wanted to please his girlfriend, he decided to ask them. His grades were certainly good enough to get into a college, and MEG (his pet name for Mary Elise Giambone) said that if he wanted to go, he would have to apply now because most schools had November cut-off dates for applicants.

After a Tuesday night Pizza from Marie's House of Tomato Pies dinner, while Farmer and Vienna sat together on the sofa drinking coffee and watching the television, Tucker sat cross-legged at their feet and asked them, "Can I go to college?" He watched their faces sag, as if they had anticipated this question long ago.

"We're sorry, Tucker. We can't afford to send you to college," his father answered. They returned to their TV program and Tucker to his homework. Game, set, match. Marine Corps, here I come.

>*The bell chimes precisely at 6:30 p.m., but they expect it since the visitor is all about discipline and punctuality. Farmer turns off the television and moves into the dining room. Vienna fluffs her hair, and the davenport pillows, and then she scurries into the kitchen to check on the coffee and brownies. Tucker goes to the door and awaits the signal from his mother that all is Ok.*
>
>*After what seems like forever, but in reality is no more than fifteen-seconds, she signals her last second inspection of the house is finished, all is in order, and she is prepared to entertain a guest, especially one as significant as this. Tucker opens the door.*
>
>*Filling the doorway is SSGT. J.D. Spurlock, USMC. He is a giant of a man, standing just over six and half-feet tall, with ice-blue eyes and a "high and tight" Marine Corps haircut. His dress blue tunic stretches wide at his shoulders and tapers down to his waist in a perfect V.*
>
>*Four vertical rows of brightly colored ribbons rise above the left breast pocket. Pinned just below the ribbons and hanging over the pocket are two silver medals; one a wreath with two crossed rifles, the other a smaller wreath with two crossed pistols. They indicate that SSGT. Spurlock is an expert shot with an M-14 rifle, and a Colt .45 pistol.*
>
>*In his right hand, he holds a briefcase. In his left, he*

holds his dress cover (Marine Corps parlance for matching hat), but not by the highly polished leather bill.

"Hi, Sergeant Spurlock," Tucker gushes. "Come on in."

The Marine recruiter steps through the door and smiles wide. "Thank you, son," he answers in a deep southern drawl. "This is surely a big night for you and your parents."

When they are all seated around the dining room table, Vienna pours coffee and serves the brownies. Tucker, wearing a dress shirt and tie for the occasion, sits next to the recruiter and across the table from his parents. Blanche, who asked permission to sit in on the historic event, sits at the end of the table with her legs curled beneath her.

The recruiter opens his briefcase, withdraws a two-inch stack of papers, and spreads them out on the table. He congratulates Tucker for successfully completing the requirements for enlistment into the Marine Corps, and especially for qualifying for early enlistment in the "120-day Plan." By doing so, Tucker can sign his enlistment contract four-months before reporting to Boot Camp, with a guaranteed start date and choice of school after graduation.

Since Tucker is only 17, his parents must co-sign the four-year contract that the recruiter has now placed in front of them. Farmer and Vienna look at one another and nod. Before they sign the government document, they each ask their son the same question. "Is this what you want to do, Tucker?"

"I'm sure," he answers.

When they finish signing their part of the contract, they slide it across the table to Tucker, who affixes his signature to the bottom of the page. He is officially the newest Marine Corps recruit and will report in July to Parris Island, South Carolina for 12 weeks of basic training.

The one tug at his heart about leaving home was that he wouldn't see his parents for three months. Tucker had never stayed away from them more than a night, except for his hospital stays, but their encouragement and support about his decision to enlist in the Marine Corps ended his separation anxiety.

Tucker's party didn't rank up there with the *bacchanalian festival* that Township Mayor Mercedes George threw for her twit son Ellis, whose sole ambition after graduation was to become a Chiropodist, and which was paid for by the good sports of the town known as the taxpayers.

There were no garden parties, Society Page newspaper columns, Negro servants, or chauffeur driven, police escorted limousines ferrying dozens of inebriated teenage partygoers from their suburban homes to a hotel suite looking out on the Manhattan skyline.

Thankfully, it also wasn't the subject of tomorrow morning's Herald headlines.

Drunken Teen Graduates trash hotel lobby in free-for-all. Seven arrested. Mayor probed.

Instead, it was the homemade version. Trays of homemade potato salad, homemade macaroni salad, homemade deviled eggs, cold cuts, fried chicken, garden salad, rolls, and assorted breads fanned out in decimated clusters across the top of the dining room table.

In the center of the table, illuminated on either side by the thick, stubby candles in Vienna's antique crystal candleholders, sat the remains of a sheet cake. Once a work of baker's art, handcrafted in chocolate batter, vanilla icing, and midnight blue trim, it was now a pathetic and skeletal wasteland of crumbs and hardened sugar. The plastic diploma, and the Marine Corps emblem, an eagle, globe, and anchor, had long been removed from the top of the cake and secured for posterity.

A white bed sheet draped over the two center dining room windows, read "Congratulations Tucker—IHS graduate '63!" The words were spray painted on in red paint. Blue and white balloons, crepe paper, and steamers hung suspended from the chandelier above the table. Half-full plastic cups, plastic plates, knives and forks littered the tabletop.

On the kitchen floor, in a metal washtub, beer for the grownups was nestled in five pounds of crushed ice: Ballantine (Farmer's brew of choice because it was Yankee's announcer Mel Allen's brew of choice), Schaeffer, and Pabst Blue Ribbon—in the can, or in the bottle, whichever you prefer. For the about-to-be-grownups, there was iced-tea, Pepsi, Save-Rite orange soda, and apple juice. Coffee and milk with dessert.

Tucker stood alone in the far corner of the dining room, between the buffet table and the China closet, arms folded across his chest, watching his party in action. He was tired and sweaty from dancing and needed a breather. Besides, the party was clearly winding down. Guests had begun trickling out about 9:00 p.m., 30-minutes ago.

The first to leave had been Father Winot (pronounced wee-no, although the Acolytes had fun calling him Father Why Not?), the diminutive, bespectacled priest from St. Andrews Episcopal, Tucker's church. Before he left, he took Tucker aside, made the sign of the cross on his forehead, and whispered, "May God bless and protect you, my son."

It was only after he departed that the music and conversation increased in volume. Mrs. Cheval followed him out the door, after kissing Tucker on the cheek and encouraging him to continue his "creative endeavors."

To Tucker's left, beyond the gaggle of revelers standing under the archway that separated the living room from the dining room, a canopy of cigarette smoke lingered near the ceiling. Beneath it, the din of conversation was barely audible over Dion's "The Wanderer," and those dancing and singing to the raucous beat.

In front of Tucker, the scene was more tranquil. Uncle Ted, Captain of a Merchant Marine vessel and rarely seen at family functions, stood off to the right, next to the swinging door that led into the kitchen. His crooked cigar bobbed up and down between his teeth while he engaged in an animated conversation with his wife, Aunt Louise, Vienna's youngest sister.

"This country is going to hell in a hand basket," he moaned. "Who do those God-less heathens in the Supreme Court think they are? Who are they to tell us we can't read the Bible or pray in schools anymore? God? I'm not kidding you, Lou. We're going down the slippery slope to moral bankruptcy. Rock 'n Roll music is filling the kids' heads with the devil; the coloreds are rioting in the South. What's next?"

Bald, stout, and minus the ring finger on his left hand, he was still an imposing figure who thrilled Tucker with war stories of drama on the high seas.

Nicky Giambone, Roger Hahn, and his brother Paul huddled on the other side of the dining room table, next to the living room archway, shoveling food into their mouths. Between bites, they, too, were speaking with subdued passion.

"Mickey Mantle is much better than Willie Mays," Paul insisted, crumbs spitting from his mouth.

"Yeah, right. You don't know your can from your elbow," Roger sniffed. "That's why Mays signed a record-breaking contract last February for $100,000."

"Mantle signed the same contract for a hundred G's a week later, so what?"

Farmer, Cousin Donny, and Max Cohen, stood only a half-dozen steps to Tucker's immediate left, and had their backs to him. Donny spoke in hushed, conspiratorial tones about his experiences in the blockade. Farmer and Max paid rapt attention, occasionally nodding, but not interrupting.

From the living room, voices suddenly erupted. The boys were singing Jimmy Soul's hit record.

*If you wanna be happy for the rest of your life,
Never make a pretty woman your wife,
So from my personal point of view,
Get an ugly girl to marry you.*

Tucker grinned. The song was funny, and he teased Mary Elizabeth every time they were together and it played on the radio. She was striking in her youthful, Mediterranean beauty. He was happy, bubbling inside, like an Alka Seltzer. The party had been a perfect way to end a perfect day.

Hungry, he grabbed a Kaiser roll, lathered it with mayonnaise, and piled it high with rare roast beef and Swiss cheese. After sprinkling a few potato chips next to it on the plate, and garnishing it with pickles, he pushed open the swinging door and sauntered into the kitchen. He was nearly knocked aside by Blanche, and her friend, Lorraine, as they dashed into the living room when they heard Lesley Gore singing, "It's My Party."

"Watch where you're going, morons," he chuckled. It felt like it was yesterday that he said the very same thing to some underclassmen. Oh, wait, he thought. It *was* yesterday.

"Come here, sweetheart," Aunt Corrine said to Tucker. "Give us a hug. We're so proud of you."

"Aye, that we are," followed Aunt Tina, Farmer and Corrine's youngest sister. "I haven't been kissed by a Marine in a long time."

"When was you kissed by a Marine, Tina? Are you hidin' somethin' from me?" slurred Uncle Bob, her burly, newly retired State Trooper husband.

"It was after the sailor and the army guy left the house," Tina winked. "The Marine snuck in just before you came home tonight and planted a big one on me. Didn't you see my smeared lipstick, you stupe? How in heaven's name did you ever catch any crooks?"

The beer had been flowing in the kitchen, and it was obvious that some of Tucker's relatives were past the point of no return. He didn't care as long as they were relatively civil. Sometimes the

Scottish blood boiled, and things got loud, but not tonight. He loved them all and was thrilled they were with him to celebrate.

Seated next to Uncle Bob was Uncle John, Aunt Corrine's husband. Tucker thought he was a very cool cat because he fawned over Tucker as if he was his own son and who bore an eerie resemblance to movie star Errol Flynn. Uncle Frank and Aunt Grace, both of whom wore their teeth (he wore his glass eyeball, too), sat with their backs against the wall.

Vienna leaned against the kitchen counter, holding a Styrofoam cup of coffee and talking to Joey Lemongello, resplendent in a gray sharkskin suit, black shirt, and white tie.

"Hey, cherryjello," Uncle Bob garbled, "what's the story on the kids? Why are they breakin' up? You have anything to do with it?"

"Lemongello. The name is Lemongello," Joey seethed. "How many times tonight do I gotta tell you?"

"Lemon jello, cherry jello, what's the difference, paisan? They both look good on the outside, but taste slimy on the way down. Capish?"

"Bob!" Vienna yelled. "You apologize right this instant! You are not in the Mob Squad anymore! CAPISH?"

"Aw, the hell with it. Sure, Joey, old pal. I apologize. Actually, I never ate lemon jello, but I look forward to it." Bob grinned, stared intently at Joey, and gulped down his beer. "So, what happened?"

Tucker still had to pinch himself. It had been almost a year since he signed with The Boys of Avon Avenue and recorded "Rock 'n Roll Knights," now charted at the number fifteen spot, with "a bullet." That meant it was on the way up the charts, with nothing to stop it—Gold record-ville.

He didn't understand why the record company waited so long to release the song. The producers were members of the Four Seasons, and, last summer they had the incredible hit song "Sherry (Baby)," just like Joey said they would.

It seemed natural that The Boys of Avon Avenue would benefit from that association, but the record executives never brought it up. Whenever Tucker questioned it, Joey told them, "Be patient, fellas. It'll come out when we say it's coming out. Until then, do your shows, collect your money, and let me handle the business."

Money? By the time the Boys paid Joey his commission, the record company for pictures, studio time, and food, and gas for the bus, they had little money remaining. They split that five ways.

The thrill of this whole thing, at least for Tucker, was not the tiny amount of money he received every 30-days, or the applause, or even being on the same stage with his teen idols. He learned early that pride and ego can be destructive. Simply, it was hearing his voice on the radio.

The first time he heard it was a few weeks ago when his radio alarm went off in the morning. He rocketed out of bed and jumped down the stairs yelling, "It's on the radio! I'm on the radio!"

Of course, the entire family flew into the kitchen and turned on WABC, and there it was—Tucker's sweet tenor voice, high-fever and all.

Now he stood next to Ruby Nash Curtis, the lead singer of Ruby and the Romantics, who currently had a smash hit, "Our Day Will Come," and peeked at the audience from the wings in the historic Apollo Theatre. They watched Redd Fox, in big shoes and oversized eyeglasses paralyze the audience with laughter. Tucker was impressed, if not assured, by the sea of black faces in the audience.

The Boys of Avon Avenue had always been popular with the colored kids, especially their hit "Rock 'n Roll Knights." That is why Tucker was confused at the polite applause, mixed with some jeering, when they finished their song.

The next morning, just before he left for school, Joey called him. "*Listen kid, the record's been pulled from the radio stations. It seems another group from Tennessee, a black group, also recorded the same song. What do you know? They're gonna sue us unless we get it off. The news was all over the radio yesterday, but I didn't want to upset you before the show. That's why I didn't tell you. I guess the kids knew it. Oh, and one more thing, the record company is dropping you guys.*"

Tucker listened impassively as Joey recounted the nightmare. He suddenly understood that another door had closed. There had also been an opportunity to get the attention of a major league baseball scout who had come to his high school game in April to see him play. He booted a routine grounder in the bottom of the 7th inning that let the winning run score, and he whiffed three times at bat. That door didn't just close, it slammed shut. Then there was college. SLAM! Finally, no hit record, no record contract, no tours. Slam, slam, slam.

"Well, it's late," Vienna interrupted, "and the all The Boys of Avon Avenue are here. Let's have one more private concert before we say goodnight."

They filed into the living room, drinks in hand, and made themselves comfortable. When everybody settled, Tucker said, "This will be our last performance." Fittingly, their final song was the Skyliners' hit, "I'll Be Seeing You." They received a standing ovation.

Tucker stood next to the door as his guests filed out. He hugged them all, collecting an interesting mosaic of lipstick prints on his cheeks. "Thank you for coming and for your gifts. I will cherish them as I do you," were his words to all. After they had all left, he leaned against the door and sighed. It was over.

While Farmer and Vienna began cleaning up, Tucker drove Mary Elise home. When he returned, all the lights were out, except for the orange nightlight in the kitchen. A hand-written note was taped to the refrigerator door.

Hi Tuck,

We couldn't keep our eyes open. I hope you aren't upset that we didn't wait up. It's been a long day for all of us, and now it's time to sleep. Before that, we want to say how proud we are of you, and how you've handled yourself growing up, becoming a man. It's never easy but you've done it with grace. Now you reap the rewards. As you enter the world, don't look back. Eat life as if it were your last meal. There is a lot of competition, but you'll find that out very shortly. We can't protect you anymore, son, but we're confident that you'll do fine. You have been a joy and a source of inspiration.

The world knows not what awaits.

PROFILE: Lesley Gore
Interview: July 24, 1990

Did the fact that you came from an upper middle-class family have anything to do with your success?

"There's nothing much to talk about in that respect. They didn't influence it. They were, in fact, not altogether for it at the time that it went down. So, they were not really influential.

"My musical influences were much stronger and go back considerably earlier than the early sixties. I guess I started listening to music when I was quite a young child. I grew up to Patti Page, Dinah Washington. These were some of the women who were popular and on the charts at the time.

"Then I discovered there were a whole group of women who, in fact, were not being played on the Pop charts but who were singing the kind of music that I really related to. These were people like June Christy, Anita O'Day, Ella Fitzgerald, and, of course, Chris Connor. I listened with tremendous fervor to these ladies.

"I considered them interpreters of lyric and, I think of my very first musical influences, that is what I tried to do. I increased my repertoire in terms of songs, but I listened to how these ladies put over a song and how they projected a lyric. That's where my very first influences in music came.

"As the '50s came into being and I would sit and do my homework listening to the Top-40 station like every other teenager in America at the time. I was listening to a simpler kind of music but slightly more raw; not quite as produced as some of the things I was listening to, and Rock 'n Roll began to effect my life.

"So, by the time I was in my mid to late teens my influences were Rock and Jazz related. Those were a perfect combination to work with a man by the name of Quincy Jones, which is ultimately, where I wound up.

"Mercury Records and, primarily, Irving Green who was the President of Mercury at the time, put me together with Quincy, very specifically, because he understood that the market was going Rock. I was a young person, and it (Jazz and Rock) could be a combination that might work. In other words, they kind of thought of me as their young Sarah Vaughn. Sarah Vaughn might not be selling the volume of records at the time that they wanted her to sell, but they thought I could hit the teen market."

As a senior in high school, your cousin Alan played a role in beginning your performing career. How did that happen?

"It was definitely the first time I got up on stage. It was the beginning for me.

"Alan was a drummer in a band, and they weren't strictly a Rock band, by the way. They played Rock, and they played romantic music. They were called upon to play a lot of catering houses in the Queens, New York area for weddings, and Bar Mitzvahs, and birthday parties, and celebrations of that kind. So, their repertoire was quite expansive, and they were putting themselves through school.

"One Sunday night, the band was playing in Queens at a catering house called Blazers and, I believe it was an Italian wedding. My cousin Alan was at my house

Lesley Gore

in Tenafly, New Jersey, at a barbecue. He got a call somewhere around six or seven o'clock that evening that the singer that was supposed to be with them that night was ill and couldn't show up. He turned around to me and said, 'Why don't you do it?' My parents weren't all that thrilled, but they knew that Alan would take good care of me, and they allowed me to go.

"It was really the first time that I understood what it was like to be a performer and sing for people. We stayed all night and did something like three or four different sets with the band, and we went through songs that we knew. It wasn't a bona fide act like I do today."

How did your career evolve from singing at Italian weddings?

"I did some more work with Alan's band whenever they needed me. They were trying to get themselves a recording contract as a band, just as a band. They booked themselves at a cocktail lounge at the Prince George Hotel, which, today, is a welfare hotel, but in the mid '60s was a nice residential hotel, and they had a lovely cocktail bar.

"They invited some record industry people down to see them. I went down that night just to be supportive. I went there with a date and, I don't know if Quincy was there, or somebody from Mercury Records, but I got up to sing with the band and somebody heard me. My demos' got to Irving Green, and he signed me and not Alan's band."

How was it decided to release "It's My Party," a definite up-tempo, pop tune, when you were signed for your Sarah Vaughn-like Jazz influence?

"Well, if you listen to the vocal interpretations, I mean I go back, and I listen to my very first album and there are songs like "Cry Me A River," and all of those songs which we did live Pop arrangements to, but the interpretations were very much coming from a young woman who was Jazz oriented to some degree.

"I don't think Quincy went out to make Sarah Vaughn records, don't misunderstand me. We were going for the teen market. When we sat down at my house on a Sunday afternoon in Tenafly, and he brought a stack of demo records, we played a lot of songs.

"Out of a pile of 200 demo records, the only song we picked that day was "It's My Party." He had chosen it out of a number of things, and then I chose it when he brought it to my house. We were very much in accord on that particular song. When I listen to "It's My Party," I can hear certain Jazz licks in the interpretation of the lyrics or at least more so than other female groups were doing in terms of singing songs at that time."

I think "You Don't Own Me" is more representative of the Jazz, Sarah Vaughn-like style. What do you think?
"I do, too, probably for a whole other set of reasons. For me, "You Don't Own Me" was probably the most powerful piece of material that I ever found and, today, it still serves as the closer to my show. That says an awful lot that after 27-years, I can't find a song that's more important, that's grown as much as I have and perhaps more, because it means more to people today than it did back in 1964. That's the test of an absolutely great song, I think. I think it's true that it could be an anthem.

"It's my Party," ... I think people remember actually where they were sitting, or standing, or what they were doing when they first heard that song. That's an interesting piece of information right there. I don't think the song, however, is as important, of course, as is "You Don't Own Me."

"In terms of "It's My Party" being a break-out single, it was the perfect song. If we opened with "You

Don't Own Me," we might not have gotten any further if people had not accepted that message from a young woman. We eased them in with "It's My Party."

"I can assure you that it was not thought out that way. When we released "It's My Party," we just thought it was a hit. We went with it, and we didn't find "You Don't Own Me" for several months down the line."

What was the transition like going from an All-American teenage girl to a celebrity?

"You have been around long enough, as have been your readers, to know that human nature is human nature. Some very lovely things happened at the time and some very difficult things happened. I very quickly at the age of 16 understood the burden of the responsibility I had taken on, and I don't say that lightly.

"I was getting mail from a lot of young people, many of whom wished they could be in the same position and some of whom probably had the talent to do the same. Nevertheless, what did disturb me was that I got a lot of letters from people who were relating to me as a young woman, and these children had a lot of problems.

"I had grown up, as you have mentioned, in a kind of secluded, cloistered world. Life wasn't perfect, but life was pretty good. I didn't have too many problems. The occasional acne, the occasional problem at school, but nothing earth shattering. I didn't have real problems.

"I started getting mail from children whose parents were alcoholics and who were being abused. Suddenly I realized that life was not what my parents had taught me it was. That was a very, very difficult time for me to see how other kids my age were being brought up in the world, because I had a very simplistic view of life.

"I had friends that remained my friends, and then there were those that just kind of jumped on because they wanted to be my friend now that I achieved something that they wanted to be a part of. That's human nature, and it happens throughout your life. I just learned it earlier than most."

Your growth as an artist was rapid as witnessed by your material. From "It's My Party," to "You Don't Know Me," to "Sunshine, Lollipops, and Rainbows," your experimentation of new styles is obvious. Was that a Quincy Jones influence or your own sense of artistic growth?

"It's interesting because "Sunshine, Lollipops, and Rainbows" was a song that we found, I would say, several months after we recorded "It's My Party." It got released after "You Don't Own Me," but it was one of the earlier pieces we did.

"The head of promotion at Mercury, a guy by the name of Morris Diamond, said that he was getting incredible reaction to "Sunshine, Lollipops, and Rainbows" from all the disc jockeys. Why? Because the record was one minute and thirty-nine seconds long.

"When they were bumping up against the news on the half-hour, or the hour, they often needed something to fill in that time, and they didn't have two-and-a-half or three minutes. They had a minute and a half. That made "Sunshine, Lollipops, and Rainbows" a hit, believe it or not."

It's been reported that your father taught you fiscal responsibility early by putting you on a $30-a-week allowance and investing the rest of your money. Is that true?

"No, it's not. I'll tell you, the financial thing is well out of proportion. Maybe one or two checks came in the early years from Mercury, and mostly they did all the recordings, so all of that got charged against me.

"Most of us know today that you don't make your money in records anyway. You make it in personal appearances. I kept them quite limited because I was in school. So, I did not amass the fortune people think I did.

"As for investing my money, it was extremely wise. Then it got lost in the stock market, so how wise could it be?"

When you moved to Los Angeles, did you simultaneously pursue an acting career?

"No, it was my desire to continue my musical career. That got me out to L.A., because, virtually, there was no industry left in New York in the midsixties. Every record company had closed their doors and moved out to the west coast. So, it almost became incumbent upon me that if I wanted to be in the music business, I had to move to either L.A., or Nashville.

"I did do some minor roles, like in the "Donna Reed Show," where I played myself. I did get the opportunity to play the Assistant to Cat Woman in the "Batman" TV series which was an awful lot of fun. I played Julie Newmar's assistant.

"But, again, I think that they were looking for someone who could sing, and we happened to have had "California Nights" out, and they wanted to incorporate that into their show. So, I think they hired me because I had those records, and they wrote the part for me.

"I did a couple of "beach" films, where I kind of lip-synced some songs. I actually felt badly that they put my name on the marquee because it often looked like I was starring in these films."

What is the significance of the performer's role in shaping our youth, and is it more important today than in the '60s?

"Today, at forty-four-years-old, I don't feel it is a burden as I did when I was sixteen. Today, I view it as a responsibility, and a part of my job, and a part of what my reason on Earth is. That is to communicate with people, to give them joy and to bring them entertainment. It is also to spread love and to spread good messages.

"Where I don't use the stage as a stand for my thoughts, I do like to incorporate what I think in my show. There are areas outside of my performance, where I do really offer a tremendous amount of time and energy, specifically women's issues, specifically pro-choice issues, and specifically the environment.

"These are the things that I'm concerned about, because I'm concerned about the next generation. That's my responsibility whether I have six kids or whether I don't. I write songs about these things. Sometimes I perform them, sometimes I don't. I have a song called "We Just Can't Walk through Life," and it's a hard-hitting song. It doesn't have any answers, but it does tell you that you just can't walk through life, you've got a responsibility."

Are your audiences allowing you to do original, current music? Are you, like so many other recording artists of the early days of Rock 'n Roll, mandated to stick to your hits?

"You know, it's interesting that you brought that up. More and more, I have, been putting in new material, or my own material mixed in with the hits, and it's been very, very well accepted. That, to me, is the key. That is primarily what I do in my show today.

"I've laid out all the hits, and I don't do them in a medley in twelve minutes. I try to do them as honestly and with as much integrity today as I did back then.

"Then I put four or five songs I've written, such as "Out Here on My Own." I sit down at the piano, very often before "It's My Party" and do, much to the surprise of the audience, all alone at the piano "Out Here on My Own." Usually, it's a very stirring Moment.

"I have another song called "America's Sweetheart" which is really an autobiography in about three minutes. It covers twenty seven years and tells what it was like to be America's sweetheart, to be up there for a minute and come down again, and where you find yourself and how you deal with it.

"Those are the kinds of things that I'm writing about now, and when I put them in front of an audience, it seems they are accepting it quite nicely."

Partial Discography
LESLIE GORE
   "It's My Party"
   "Judy's Turn to Cry"
   "You Don't Own Me"
   "Sunshine, Lollipops, and Rainbows"
   "Maybe I know"
   "That's the Way Boys Are"

EPILOG

"I'll be looking at the moon, but I'll be seeing you."

July, 1963

1.

Tucker walked briskly across the Newark Airport tarmac, mingling in with the other passengers bound for Charleston, South Carolina. The brutal humidity was already in full force, and rivers of sweat trickled down his face. He took off his sports jacket and slung it over his shoulder, but by the time he bounded up the metal stairs and boarded the National Airlines DC-3, he was drenched. I'd better learn to love the heat and humidity, he thought. Where I'm heading, it's much worse.

He shuffled down the aisle and found his seat next to the window, directly behind the port engine. Once settled, he pulled the sealed envelope from his coat jacket and fingered it open. His father had asked him not to read it until he was on the plane.

Hi Tucker,

Just a few reminders. First, you have to look at yourself in the mirror every day when you shave, so you'd better like what you do for your life's work. Next, you enter the adult world with only your name. How you behave in life will determine what your name stands for. Finally, don't forget the message of 1 Corinthians 13:11—

When I was a child, I spoke like a child.
I thought like a child.
When I became a man, I put aside childish things.

I expect big things from you, Tucker. Set a goal to be the best Marine out of Boot Camp. You know you can do it. Keep your mouth shut, do exactly what you are told, and do it better than anyone else. I am proud of you, and I love you.
Semper Fi!
Dad

Tucker folded the note and replaced it in the envelope just as the two huge Pratt and Whitney propellers began to turn. He glanced out the window and saw his parents and Mary Elise standing at the observation deck. Farmer and Vienna held hands and waved. Mary Elise held a cardboard sign and pressed it against the window. It read, "I Love you, Tucker. I'll wait for you."

For an instant, he felt an overwhelming urge to shout for the plane to stop and let him get off. It had all been a big mistake. The feeling passed quickly, however, and as the plane taxied away from the terminal, he waved and smiled. In minutes, the DC-3 roared down the runway and lifted off gently into the mid-morning sky.

As the ground receded, Tucker relaxed and enjoyed the thrill of seeing the Manhattan skyline *below him.* The plane banked right in a slow southerly maneuver and climbed to its cruising altitude of 23,000 feet. As it leveled, the sun flooded into the cabin and reflected brilliantly off the Atlantic Ocean below.

"It's a glorious day, isn't it?" whispered the elderly woman sitting next to him.

"Yes, it sure is," he answered.

"What's your name?"

"I'm Tucker Pitts, ma'am."

"Where are you headed?"

"Well, you see, I just graduated from high school and ..."

2.

The Presidential News Conference was thick with journalists all competing for President Kennedy's attention. From the middle of the room, a reporter asked, "Mr. President, there has been a good deal of public concern about the political situation in South Vietnam, and I would like to ask you whether the difficulties between the Buddhist population there and the South Vietnamese Government has been an impediment to the effectiveness of American aid in the war against the Viet Cong?"

"Yes, I think it has," the President replied. "I think it is unfortunate that this dispute has arisen at the very time when the military struggle has been going better than it has been going in many months.

"I would hope that some solution could be reached for this dispute, which certainly began as a religious dispute, and because we have invested a tremendous amount of effort and it is going quite well.

He continued, "I would hope this would be settled, because we want to see a stable government there, carrying on a struggle to maintain its national independence. We strongly believe in that. We are not going to withdraw from that effort. In my opinion, for us to withdraw from that effort would mean a collapse not only of South Vietnam, but of Southeast Asia. So, we are going to stay there ..."

The Beginning